HITLER YOUTH ATTACKS!

Recent Titles by Leo Kessler from Severn House

Writing as Leo Kessler

S.S.Wotan Series
Assault On Baghdad
Death's Eagles
The Great Escape
Kill Patton
Operation Glenn Miller
Patton's Wall
The Screaming Eagles
Sirens of Dunkirk
Wotan Missions

Battle for Hitler's Eagles' Nest
The Blackout Murders
The Churchill Papers
Murder at Colditz
The Blackout Murders

Writing as Duncan Harding

Assault on St Nazaire
Attack New York!
The Finland Mission
Hell on the Rhine
The Normandie Mission
Operation Judgement
Sink the Ark Royal
Sink the Bismarck
Sink the Cossack
Sink the Graf Spee
Sink HMS Kelly
Sink the Hood
Sink the Prince of Wales
Sink the Scharnhorst
Sink the Tirpitz
Sink the Warspite
Slaughter in Singapore
The Tobruk Rescue

HITLER YOUTH ATTACKS!

Leo Kessler

severn
House

This first world edition published in Great Britain 2004 by
SEVERN HOUSE PUBLISHERS LTD of
9–15 High Street, Sutton, Surrey SM1 1DF.
This first world edition published in the USA 2004 by
SEVERN HOUSE PUBLISHERS INC of
595 Madison Avenue, New York, N.Y. 10022.

British Library Cataloguing in Publication Data

Kessler, Leo, 1926-
    Hitler Youth attacks!. - (S. S. Wotan series)
    1.   World War, 1939-1945 - Campaigns - Fiction
    2.   War stories
    I.   Title
    823.9'14 [F]

    ISBN 0-7278-6089-5

Typeset by Palimpsest Book Production Ltd.,
Polmont, Stirlingshire, Scotland.
Printed and bound in Great Britain by
MPG Books Ltd., Bodmin, Cornwall.

BOOK ONE

The Baby Division

But here we are again like men redeemed from the grave . . . We gave death the chance. Death did not take us and we escaped alive.

Siegfried Sassoon

One

B ehind them, as the long troop train began to slow down, the snow-capped mountains of Russia started to disappear. Now on both sides of the track, the fields, untended ever since 1941, were free of snow, though the rusting tanks and burned-out trucks still bore out testimony to those first victorious battles of that summer. Behind them the German sappers would soon be busy blowing up the switch line the train was using. Everywhere the *Wehrmacht* was in retreat. The survivors of SS Assault Regiment Wotan had seen the last of Russia. Now they were going home to defend the Reich, and although that involved yet more fighting, they were glad to be doing so. For as the red-faced Sergeant Schulze, seated on the lice-ridden dirty straw next to crackling, red-glowing oven, roared, raising his 'flatman' in a toast, '*Dosvedanya Russiya* . . . Goodbye, you frigging Popovs . . . We're not coming back, *tovarichi*.'

Although the survivors envied the big burly sergeant the fiery vodka he was swallowing greedily, they yelled his toast: '*Goodbye, you frigging Popovs . . . we're not coming back!*'

Corporal Matz, Schulze's long-time running mate, said, 'Come on, Schulzi, save me a drop o' that frigging fire-water, you greedy bugger. You've nearly finished the flatman.'

Schulze paused, gasping a little for breath. 'What does it matter, Matzi – and remember, you puny aspagarus Tarzan, to show some respect for a senior NCO.'

'Go and piss in the wind,' Matz retorted.

3

Schulze was happy – and half drunk. He ignored the comment. Instead he said pleasantly, 'I am now empowered to tell you on the highest authority that when we stop, comrades, we shall be welcomed by no less a person than old Father Christmas hissen.'

There was a gasp of surprise from the bearded, weary veterans. *'Father Christmas!'* they exclaimed with delight.

Schulze's big red face cracked into a huge, tough smile. 'Yessir. And you know what kind of Christmas presents he'll have for us.' He swallowed the rest of his vodka with a flourish. 'Booze and beaver.' He grabbed the front of his trousers as if he were in some considerable pain. 'And Frau Schulze's handsome son hasn't had a bit o' beaver ever since he won number five place in the queue for that whore in Smolensk. And I could only pleasure her twice in five minutes.' He shook his big cropped head. 'I swear, if this goes on, I'll be impotent before 1944 is over . . .'

As the train slowed ever more, 'Pill', as the regimental surgeon of what was left of SS Assault Regiment Wotan was known, reached for his helmet and his little black bag, watched from the opposite seat by Kuno von Dodenburg. Short-arm inspection, Pill?' he asked a little wearily. After all, the last two weeks had been hell. He had lost half his regiment, especially the 'greenbeaks', the teenage reinforcements to Wotan. Now all he had left were his 'old hares', his veterans, who had known how to look after themselves and each other even in the thick of the fighting retreat.

'Yes, the boys, if you can call those half-cripples of yours, Kuno, "boys", deserve a bit of fun. I'll have a quick look at Father Christmas's – er – ladies.' He grinned at the regimental commander. 'I wouldn't want our men infecting our German virgins with some kind of social disease.'

Kuno von Dodenburg returned his grin. 'Yes, that would be unfortunate. We must protect our virginal womenfolk from the licentious soldiery at all costs. The Führer expects it of us.'

Pill nodded, touched his hand casually to the rim of his helmet and prepared to leave the officer's compartment. Von Dodenburg stopped him hastily. 'You've forgot your pistol, Pill,' he reminded the middle-aged doctor of medicine. 'Remember, we're not out of the wood yet, old house.'

'Thanks, Kuno. But remember I'm supposed to heal human beings, not shoot 'em.'

'Remember, too, Pill, that we're not quite out of the land of the Popovs yet. Here anything can happen – and usually does.'

As the train came to a halt, Pill nodded and, pulling up his collar against the biting wind which came straight from Siberia, stepped outside into the freezing cold.

Father Christmas was waiting for him. He came to attention awkwardly and reported in traditional army fashion: 'Mobile Brothel Number Fifteen ready for inspection, sir. Twelve whores and five German service personnel present and correct, sir.'

Pill didn't even bother to return the salute. He smiled at 'Father Christmas', who had got his name from his benign appearance, shock of white hair and sizeable paunch, and said, 'Hello, you old rogue. Still suffering for the Führer, eh?' He tapped the NCO's paunch, which threatened to burst out of his grey *Wehrmacht* tunic at any moment.

Sergeant Habermann, the keeper of 'Mobile Brothel Number Fifteen', returned his smile and said, 'We must do our utmost for our brave fighting boys, sir. Nothing's too good for them. That's the least older soldiers like me can do.'

'Of course and old slit-ear that you are, you haven't been doing so badly for yourself either.' The Pill was businesslike again. 'All right, any pox to report?'

'No, sir. I keep my girls clean, sir. They're good hard-working wenches.' He indicated the handful of bored-looking whores who were hanging out of the windows of the shell-pocked railway building opposite, smoking moodily as they waited for the next batch of customers. 'Even if they are all

Polacks. Serviced a whole battalion of spaghetti-eaters last week.' Father Christmas meant Italians. 'They done 'em in two hours flat, and everybody knows how them dagoes like their gash.'

Pill nodded. 'Right, I'll have a quick look at my chaps. Get your ladies on their backs ready to dance the Mattress Polka. We haven't got too much time. The Ivans are not that far off.'

Father Christmas's broad smile vanished momentarily. 'How far, sir? I mean we aren't combatants and I must protect my girls. They say those Ivans are so randy they'd screw anything with hair on.'

'More than likely,' Pill agreed and blew his whistle sharply before crying, 'Get fell in for short-arm inspection.'

'Tell 'em, sir, please that the price has gone up. Good whores are getting very hard to find these days, especially when you want 'em to work for the Greater German *Wehrmacht*.'

Pill ignored the fat brothel-keeper, for already the Wotan veterans were streaming out of their boxcars, fumbling with their flies, yelling wildly, grasping their testicles, moaning as if in the throes of unbearable ecstasy. Even the cripples such as 'One Ball', who had part of his plumbing shot off at Leningrad, ran with the rest. Pill shook his head. How life at the front had brutalized them, he thought. Their lives were short and violent. What else could one expect of these young men, whose lives could be cut short at any moment?

Kuno von Dodenburg sat in the railway station's office while the bespectacled clerk sorted through the various travel orders, signals and the like which he would sign for as soon as the long troop train was ready to move again. Outside all was hectic activity. Ragged, emaciated Poles were carrying supplies to the train. Others were loading coal and wood for the long journey across Occupied Poland till they reached the Reich, where, von Dodenburg hoped, he and his men would be granted a well-earned rest and time to reinforce his battered regiment. Further off, his veterans were lining up and were lifting their shirts at Pill's command to 'lift the curtain' before he commenced his 'short-arm inspection'.

Despite the freezing cold, the men of Wotan didn't hesitate. With their trousers and underpants around their ankles, they raised their shirt fronts and Pill commenced his inspection of their genitals, pausing here and there when he wasn't altogether satisfied and lifting the man's penis delicately with the end of his pencil. Finally he turned to a beaming Father Christmas, already rubbing his palms together in anticipation of the money to come. 'All right, you rogue, they're all officially certified as clean and fit for human consumption. They're all yours now. Wheel 'em away.'

Again Father Christmas swung Pill one of his sloppy salutes before addressing the impatient old hares with: 'Now pin this behind yer lugs. No pushing, no shoving. Everybody's gonna get a go at my girls. But *one go only*. And all of yer'll use a Parisian.' He meant a contraceptive. 'No Parisian, no jiggy-jiggy. Got it? I'm not having one of my girls finding she's got a bun in the oven 'cos you buggers haven't taken precautions.'

'No fun wearing an overcoat made of rubber, Sarge,' someone commented.

Father Christmas overheard the remarks but Schulze growled, 'Get a move on, *Kumpel*. My outside plumbing's beginning to freeze up.'

'Never mind, Sarge,' Father Christmas said. 'My girls'll make an Egyptian mummy perform. Now then, on my word of command turn smartly to the right, with yer money in your left hand and your Parisian in yer right. Right . . . *right turn*!'

Von Dodenburg shook his head in mock wonder. In this fourth year of total war, even sex had become regimented, carried out by numbers with military precision. What a world! Then he dismissed Father Christmas and his randy 'clients' and waited impatiently for the bespectacled clerk to reappear with the more secret instructions. In particular, he was eager to know their final destination after Berlin and their posting. He prayed that it would be to remotest Bavaria, Bad Tölz or Grafenwöhr: Somewhere rural, far away from the Reich's bombed cities and the permanent reminder that Germany was losing the war rapidly.

He yawned. It was damnably hot in the little office. As usual these rear-echelon stallions, Father Christmas, his clerk and the like, knew how to make themselves comfortable. No freezing foxholes for them where front swine frequently froze to death if they weren't wakened every couple of hours and told to slap some warmth into their skinny underfed bodies. Still, von Dodenburg told himself, it was pleasant, very pleasant. And there was the delightful smell of frying potatoes, *Bratkartoffeln* done in goose fat – the kind he hadn't eaten these many months – coming from the little kitchen across the passage. He yawned again. God, it was hard work, trying to keep awake.

Outside it was growing dark. Already he could make out the shape of a sickle moon on the horizon over the bleak waste of Russia. Soon the clerk would have to black out the windows. Even here on the border between Russia and German-occupied Poland the partisans, those treacherous bastards who slaughtered lone German soldiers all the time, would be operating.

The tall, lean SS officer, his face honed to a death's head, yawned for the third time. The laughter, the cries, the chatter from the mobile brothel across the way receded into the distance. It grew silent. There was no noise now save for the spectral whisper of the night wind in the black, spiky trees.

Von Dodenburg's eyes closed. He told himself he'd open them the moment the clerk came in with the secret orders. Yes, in that very same instant. Slowly he drifted off into an untroubled sleep, his body perfectly still, his chest barely rising. A casual observer entering the room at that moment might well have thought that the SS officer was dead . . .

Outside, the dark shapes led their horses forward by the halter. They made hardly any sound. But then the riders were experts in attacks of this kind. All metal in the harnesses of their mounts had been covered and they had wound sacking around the horses' hooves. Even the blades of their curved sabres had been bandaged to prevent any noise. Now they moved along the border track which led to where the 'silent ones', the *nmetski*, were indulging in their swinish rutting like the wild animals that they were, unaware that this was the last time they would do so.

They passed a burnt-out *isba*, a peasant hut. Next to it three naked bodies hung from the skeletal trees, frozen to stone, their tongues hanging out like dried, blackened leather. One of the three was a heavy-bosomed woman, her bare breasts drooping down to her waist. Some joker among the Germans who had murdered the peasants had attached small cowbells to her nipples. Now as the bodies moved slightly in the night breeze they gave off a faint tinkling sound. The Cossacks said nothing. But their jaws hardened and their hands gripping their sabres tightened. Up front, their leader raised his hand, fingers outstretched. The riders knew what that meant. In five minutes they would attack. Silently, one after another, they swung themselves into the saddles of their wiry little ponies and started to pluck the bandages from their sabres.

Over at that remote border railway station, the old hares of SS Assault Regiment Wotan danced their wild Mattress Polkas and on the sofa in that hot little room Colonel von Dodenburg snored softly, out to the world.

Two

'*URRAH . . . URRAH . . .*' The hoarse, bass cry, followed by the thunder of galloping horses, woke von Dodenburg at once. He almost fell from the sofa where he had dozed off. He realized immediately what was happening. Under the cover of darkness the station was being attacked. Probably it was by one of the wandering Cossack bands, supported by the local partisans who supplied them with their intelligence about German activities behind the front.

But there was no time to worry about that now. Action – urgent action – was needed at once. He pulled out his whistle and shrilled three blasts on it as the thunder of the galloping hooves grew ever closer. Next instant he rushed to the window. He flung it open. Dark shapes were riding hell-for-leather across the steppe, their raised sabres gleaming silver in the light of the sickle moon. He pulled out his pistol and aimed three wild shots at the leading riders. One of the enemy was lifted clean out of his saddle by the impact of the 9mm slug slamming into his chest. He screamed and fell to the ground under the trampling hooves of the following riders.

Still the others came on, carried forward by the unreasoning blood lust of battle. Von Dodenburg fired another couple of hasty, unaimed shots and then doubled to the back of the office. Just in time. A salvo from a Russian tommy gun ripped the length of the wall where he had just been standing. Plaster and wood splinters flew everywhere. '*Clerk,*' he yelled. 'Bring me those papers . . . *Dalli . . . dalli!*'

There was no answer. Now, as everywhere in the mobile

10

brothel, women screamed and men cursed as they sought to find their weapons, some of them running into the night to take up the battle in their shirt tails. Von Dodenburg slammed open the door to the clerk's room. The clerk lay on the floor, his glasses set at a comical angle on his dead face. But there was nothing comical about the great jagged slash across his skinny throat, from which the blood was oozing a bright red.

'*Himmel, Arsch und Wolkenbruch!*' von Dodenburg cursed. They had slit the poor bastard's throat while he had slept. He would have been next if he had not been woken by the roar of the Cossacks' charging. Hastily he bent and scooped up the papers on the floor marked in crimson letters, 'Top Secret. By Officer Courier Only.' They would be the ones referring to the survivors' posting. They'd need those orders if they ever got out of this damned trap in one piece.

He stuffed them inside his tunic and as he did so, he became aware that he was not alone.

Whoever it was had made no noise, as he had done when he had slit the poor bastard of a clerk's throat. But his smell gave him away. It was typically Russian. Unmistakable: a combination of garlic, sweat and that coarse black tobacco the Popovs smoked.

Von Dodenburg swallowed hard. What was he to do? The Popov was somewhere behind him. If he picked up his pistol which he had placed on the floor to gather up the top-secret papers, the Russian would act. He'd never reach the weapon. But he couldn't crouch there much longer. The Cossacks were already beginning to fling themselves from their ponies and were rushing forward on foot, firing from the hip as they did so. Time was running out for him. Fast!

Outside, someone cried in Russian, 'Torch this building . . . *davai davai!*' It was the signal von Dodenburg needed. He *had* to act now and he did. He lashed out with his right foot. His steel-shod heel connected with human flesh. There was a cry of pain. Von Dodenburg hesitated no longer. He sprang round. In the light of the flames already beginning to spread outside as the whooping Cossacks began to set fire to the building, he saw the bearded, wolfish face of the partisan who had murdered the clerk. The man looked scared.

'*Bastard!*' von Dodenburg yelled and aimed another kick at the Russian. Von Dodenburg was in luck. He caught the man directly in the crotch. The Russian shrieked with the agony of the blow. His stainless-steel false teeth bulged from his mouth as he started to vomit, body doubled up. Von Dodenburg didn't give him a chance to recover. As the man bent, face stuck forward, von Dodenburg's knee cracked into his chin. He went staggering back. Von Dodenburg grabbed his pistol. Without taking aim, the tall SS officer loosed off a single shot. The murderer gasped with the shock of that terrible impact. His eyes rolled upwards. In the moment of his death agony, he slid slowly to the floor, tracing a path of his own blood against the whitewashed wall.

Hastily von Dodenburg slid another magazine into his pistol. Gasping now as if he had just run a great race, sweating heavily despite the night cold, he clutched the secret papers tightly to his chest and stepped outside.

To his right, his old hares had taken up the challenge. He could hear that big rogue Sergeant Schulze crying at the top of his voice, 'All right, me lucky lads, hands off yer cocks and on with yer socks,' in between firing short bursts from his Schmeisser machine pistol to left and right.

Von Dodenburg nodded his approval. The men were reacting like the seasoned veterans that they were. Still, if they were going to escape, the men would have to cover about a hundred metres before they reached the relative safety of the train, which had already raised steam, the driver and his mate still safe behind the steel plating of their cab. And the Popovs, at least twenty of the fur-hatted Cossack riders, were wheeling their ponies about and heading for the stalled troop train. They had to be stopped. But how?

For a moment or two, von Dodenburg crouched there in the

glowing darkness, wondering what he should do. He couldn't tackle twenty-odd Russians, armed only with his pistol and the mere nine rounds that its magazine contained. But von Dodenburg hadn't reckoned with Schulze and his old hares. They had seen the danger too. Now 'beaver and booze' were forgotten totally. Their lives were at stake. If they were cut off in the brothel, that would be that. SS that they were, the Popovs wouldn't show the least mercy; they'd be slaughtered out of hand.

Now as von Dodenburg crouched there, still undecided about his course of action, Schulze, his flies wide open, gave the old infantry hand signal – fist pumped up and down three times, for rally on me. Not waiting to see if the men behind would, he started to move forward. Crouched low like some Western gunslinger in an American cowboy film, he fired controlled bursts to left and right, trying to keep the Cossacks at bay. Here and there he hit a Popov, but that was not his concern at the moment. He wanted to get as many men as possible safely back to the train. Once they were aboard again there were machine guns on the roof which would keep the attackers at bay until the locomotive moved off.

Instinctively the old hares started to form a 'grape', the infantry assault formation, behind the lone NCO as he led the way, firing to left and right, taking casualties now, but giving them too. Von Dodenburg rose to his feet, his steely-blue eyes full of admiration for his men. No other unit in the whole of the Greater German *Wehrmacht* could have reacted so swiftly and so correctly as they were, caught literally with their pants down.

Now he waited no longer. He slipped to the flank of his men advancing under fire to the train. He guessed the Ivans could concentrate on them – and the mobile brothel, from which the screams of the whores being raped now started to come. He slipped down the side of the building like a ghost. His every nerve tingled electrically, but he was in control of himself. He'd been through this kind of bloody business often enough in these last terrible years. An Ivan staggered drunkenly out of the side door. He stopped instinctively, hand gripping his pistol, abruptly wet with sweat. But the Russian hadn't seen him. Cursing, '*Boshe mei*,' he opened the flies of his breeches and let loose a stream of hot urine. Breaking wind noisily for good measure, he staggered back into the building. Hastily von Dodenburg moved on. The end of the train was only twenty or thirty metres away now.

Inside his compartment, Pill ignored the slugs pattering off the metal sides of the carriage. He knew he had to do something before the men in the open were slaughtered by the advancing Russians. All the same, he told himself, he was a doctor. He was supposed to heal men, not to kill them. But what did moral dilemmas matter in this terrible war in Russia? Morality had been long thrown out of the window. Even chaplains went armed in Russia. Quarter was neither expected nor given on both sides. He made up his mind. He reached up for the trap in the compartment which led to the roof of the train and the machine guns that were positioned there in the makeshift steel turret just behind the locomotive's cab. Gasping a little with the effort and telling himself he was really getting too old for frontline duty, Pill started to crawl along the slippery roof, as below, the battle raged with ever increasing fury.

Schulze slammed his big boot into a Russian's belly, crying hoarsely, 'Try that one for collar size, you horrible man!'

The bearded Russian didn't like it. The tremedous blow raised him off his feet and propelled him several metres backwards. He hit the ground hard and didn't get up. Schulze laughed uproariously and yelled, 'Come on, you heroes, do you want to live for ever?' They didn't. It was no use telling that to Sergeant Schulze. He was too carried away with the battle to reach the train. He wouldn't have heard anyway. For the racket was tremendous, as the rush for the safety of the train deterioriated into a series of single actions, with man pitted against man: men swaying back and forth,

14

cursing obscenely, foaming at the mouth, hacking, gouging, chopping, slicing, kicking, using boots, bayonets, rifle butts to overcome the enemy in a panicked frenzy of mass mayhem.

Up on the roof now, poised behind the old-fashioned Hotchkiss machine gun, Pill eyed the throng swaying back and forth, leaving a carpet of their dead behind, as the flames from the burning brothel grew higher and higher, illuminating that terrible scene in their blood-red light. How was he going to tell friend from foe in such a confused mêlée? Still he knew he had to – and soon. For already on the horizon he could see the stark, black silhouettes of more riders galloping to the battlefield. The Russians were sending in reinforcements. In minutes they'd be joining the attack and that would be the end of what was left of SS Assault Regiment Wotan.

He felt around the old World War One machine gun, remembering his days as a young lieutenant of infantry in that forgotten war. Nothing had changed. He pulled up the sight and pressed the firing hammer. At once the gun started to chatter like an irate woodpecker. Tracer hissed through the glowing darkness like lethal Morse. Hastily he swung the gun round, firing over the heads of the Wotan men into the ranks of the attacking Russians.

They were bowled over like ninepins. Caught completely by surprise by this burst of murderous fire coming from the roof of the train, the Cossacks seemed almost to accept what was happening, as if it had been ordained by some God on high, pausing in their tracks, letting this terrible thing happen to them, falling in great bloody heaps almost without a cry of pain. Even as he fired, Pill wondered yet again at the nature of man. How could some men be so cowardly and flinch at the slightest pain, while others accepted absolute agony stoically without even a cry of anger at the terrible thing that was happening to them?

Schulze and his hard-pressed old hares had no time for such philosophical considerations. 'Good old pox doctor!' Schulze yelled happily, realizing that it had to be Pill who was firing the M.G. 'Yer can give me a short-arm inspection any time you like . . . *Los, Männer* . . . We've got the Popovs on the run . . . *Los*.' He sprang over a pile of Russian corpses, heaped together like a mess of bloody offal in a butcher's backyard, and then he was running all out, arms working like pistons, as if the Devil himself was after him . . .

Three

'*POLACKS!*' they exclaimed, as the doors of the boxcars were opened, at last letting in the fresh air and the cries of those waiting all along the track. Everywhere there were men, women and children in dirty rags, holding out their skinny claws of hands as they begged for bread in Polish and German, '*Chleb . . . Brot . . . Bitte . . . BROT!*' Here and there were women, suckling babes clutched to empty breasts, who were crying in their hunger. There were others who went down on their knees, wringing their raised hands in the classic pose of supplication.

Some of the old hares were moved enough to rummage in their bread bags and throw the Poles whatever stale crusts they still had left there. But most of them were in too much of a hurry to carry out their natural functions to worry about the Poles. They had been locked in ever since they had escaped from the trap at the mobile brothel. Now the 'piss buckets' were overflowing. They had no time to waste. Madly they swarmed out of the boxcars, pushed their way through the begging Poles and scrambled up the nearest embankment to meet the urgent call of nature. The Poles turned and began to beg from them as they squatted, exposing their naked backsides, groaning and straining, not caring that, in some cases, they were surrounded by women and children.

'The New Order,' Pill commented cynically as he and von Dodenburg strolled the length of the track, smoking cigars and enjoying the fresh air after the stuffy, fetid atmosphere on the train. 'The benefits of our glorious One Thousand

17

Years' Empire bestowed on the grateful natives, eh, Kuno.' The middle-aged doctor, with his sabre-scarred face from his student duelling days, took the cheap cigar from his mouth and added, 'Look at that.' He indicated a barefoot, swollen-bellied boy with his eyes bulging from his emaciated features rummaging in the trash thrown out of the officers' compartment. 'That Polack boy has learned from us. Officers have more food – and better – than private soldiers. Without us Germans, how could he ever have learned that, eh?'

Kuno von Dodenburg frowned. He didn't like to hear his old friend talk like this. But he didn't want to make the point that such defeatist talk was dangerous – highly dangerous. So he joked, 'They say the Polacks didn't have a pot to piss in before the war and our arrival.'

'Maybe,' Pill agreed. 'But at least they could piss when and where they liked and not when and where we, the masters, said they could. 'He shot his companion a hard look out of the side of his eyes, but von Dodenburg's face revealed nothing save that he was preoccupied with something: something which had engaged his thoughts, Pill realized, ever since he had opened their top-secret orders after escaping from the Cossacks. He wondered what it was.

For a few moments they walked in silence. Out to the rear of the train, the kitchen bulls had set up their goulash cannon. Smoke was already pouring from the blackened chimney and the cooks in their dirty whites were throwing in bricks of dried peas, which would be followed soon by rings of sausage. Together they were to form the basis for Wotan's celebrated 'Giddy-up Soup', the strongest and best soup in the whole of the Armed SS. It was reported that once, the Führer himself had tasted it and had been so entranced that he had sworn he might give up his celebrated addiction to vegetarianism because he had been so impressed. Whether that was true or not, no one was quite sure, but it was well known throughout the Black Guards that half a litre of Wotan's Giddy-up Soup could keep the average SS trooper breaking wind solidly for at least twenty-four hours. As Sergeant Schulze had once expressed it in his customary unique manner, 'A dose of that pea soup and you could fart yersen right off to heaven.'

Now the starving Poles must have thought the same. The humble peasants in their ragged clothes stood in a circle around the well-fed, crimson-faced kitchen bulls savouring the delightful smell of Giddy-up Soup while the cooks dipped and emptied their ladles of the thick dark-green liquid like artists performing in front of an enchanted audience.

Pill frowned.

Von Dodenburg caught the look. 'What is it?' he asked.

'Don't like those cooks playing games like that. I have no love for the Polacks, but there is no cause to torture their womenfolk and children with the sight of food that they're not going to get.' Pill crooked a finger at Sergeant Schulze, who, with his running mate Corporal Matz, was naturally standing first in line for his share of the celebrated soup. 'Schulze, deal with those kitchen bulls. See that they don't play any more games in front of the Polacks.'

'Yessir,' Schulze said smartly, a big grin that boded no good for the cooks spreading across his broad red face. 'I'll take care of it personally, sir.'

Pill touched his hand to his cap languidly, as Schulze threw him up a tremendous salute. The officers passed on. Von Dodenburg waited till the two officers were out of earshot, then he said, 'Pill, you mustn't take all these things so damned seriously. These Polacks and the like. In due course, I expect that we Germans might well be in the same boat, begging from out Allied conquerors.'

Again the doctor threw his companion a sidelong glance and for the first time he recognized that von Dodenburg's harshly handsome face was marred by the bitter, downturned lips of a man who had been disappointed somehow in life. But he made no comment and let von Dodenburg continue to talk.

'Pill,' he went on, 'my principles started to go out of the

window when we invaded Russia back in the summer of 1941. I knew almost immediately that we had made the wrong decision. But the Führer had decided and we followed. There was no alternative. From that time onwards my main concern has been the regiment and the survival of our men. The greater issues and the morality of what we do are no concern of mine. My aim is to bring through as many of our people as I can. They'll be sorely needed in the years to come.'

Pill laughed a little cynically. 'Yes, but the boys say, "Enjoy the war, the peace is going to be terrible."'

Von Dodenburg laughed too. 'They're probably right. But that will be only for a short time. But they will have survived – I hope.' He broke off and bit his bottom lip, as if he had suddenly been struck by an unpleasant thought. He gave a little shudder.

'A louse run over your liver?' Pill asked.

'Something like that.'

'Can you tell me, Kuno?' Pill asked in his kindly, almost avuncular manner.

'Wish I could. It would be a relief in a way to talk about it with someone else.'

'Is it to do with our posting – those secret orders?' Pill prompted.

But Kuno von Dodenburg didn't seem to hear the question and so they passed on in silence . . .

'Kuno, my boy,' his father, the general, had barked the day before the Regiment had set off for Russia for the last time, 'let's look facts in the face, what.'

Kuno had been amused. His father had always been 'looking facts in the face' ever since he could remember. Now *der Alte*, the 'old one', as he was known to all and sundry, was doing so again, as he sat in the saddle he used instead of his chair, swinging his old cavalry sabre as if he were ready for the charge.

They had met for the last time in the shabby hall of the old family home, looked down on by the yellowing portraits of his ancestors, laden with wigs and beards, all of them wearing uniform without exception. For the von Dodenburgs had always been soldiers, right back to the days of 'Old Fritz',* serving the Prussian crown and later the Imperial crown, loyal unto death. He had known why *der Alte* had summoned him to the shabby, cold hall. One, because General von Dodenburg didn't want anyone to hear what he had to say (these days even old family retainers couldn't be trusted) and, two, because the General wanted to impress upon his son the traditions of his family.

In his no-nonsense manner, General von Dodenburg had continued with a brisk, 'It can't go on, Kuno. It simply can't.'

Naturally Kuno von Dodenburg was long accustomed to his father's ways; Prussian generals, on the whole, never wasted a word. They were always brisk and to the point; sometimes too much so. 'What can't go on, Father?' he had asked a little wearily.

'This damned blood-letting. That man –' the way the General usually referred to Hitler – 'has to go. If he doesn't go soon, then there will be little left of our army and our beloved country.' The General had coughed thickly – Kuno had been able to hear the thick turgid fluid in the old General's lungs and he had realized just how old his father was.

'Father,' he had said, looking cautiously to left and right, as all Germans did these days to check whether they were being overheard, 'you mustn't talk like that. It's dangerous.'

'Dangerous be damned, Kuno,' his father had snorted. 'What can the authorities do to an old bugger like me. I won't last the damned years out as it is. You know that!'

'Don't say that, Father, please.'

The General had ignored his objection. His thin father with his drooping white cavalry moustache had flushed unhealthily. 'We von Dodenburgs have always been loyal

*Frederick the Great.

to the very end, even in defeat, Kuno,' he had rasped, 'but this situation can't go on. We are being led by a madman. The time has come to put an end to it – I won't mince words, Kuno – I mean *him*. If we don't –' he had shrugged his thin shoulders, suddenly seeming helpless – 'God help our Fatherland.'

Kuno von Dodenburg had been unable to conceal his monumental sense of shock. 'You mean get rid of the Führer?'

'Yes, I do.'

'Then?' he had asked, unable to say more.

'Then we sue for an immediate peace.' The General had frowned. 'I don't know about the Reds, but definitely with the Tommies and those other people from the New World who're fighting with them.' He clicked his fingers together impatiently. 'You know – the Americans. Sue for peace before they invade Europe. For once they do, Kuno, they won't stop until they reach Berlin and then the time for talking will be long over. We will be the defeated with no power and no rights.' He paused and Kuno had been able to hear his harsh breathing like the sound cracked bellows make. His father had been right; he wouldn't last out the year.

Now as Kuno strode the length of the platform next to an equally silent Pill, ignoring the pleas and cries of the Polacks begging for food and the noise that Schulze was making as he threatened to 'make sows' of the fat, perspiring 'kitchen bulls', he pondered the old man's words. He knew where they were going and what their task would be there. He knew, too, that would be exactly what his father, the General, didn't want him to do. But how could he avoid doing his duty and carrying out his orders, even if they meant plunging Germany into defeat at the hands of the victorious Anglo-Americans? He was an SS officer who had sworn an oath to remain 'loyal unto death'. Besides, there would have to be many more of the same inclination if they were going to succeed in the unthinkable: bringing to an end the rule of the Führer, Adolf Hitler.

'Come on, you filthy hash-slingers,' Schulze was crying at

the 'kitchen bulls', 'get on with your duties, or by the Great God of the SS and all his angels, I'll show you how to make a handsome frigging corpse!'

Kuno von Dodenburg smiled thinly despite his worries. 'Get on with your duties and make a handsome frigging corpse!' That sounded as good a motto as any for a hard-pressed SS officer in this year of defeat, 1944. Abruptly he felt quite happy.

Four

'Holy frigging strawsack!' One Ball exclaimed, as the long troop train slowly started to draw into the French station. 'As I live and breathe, is such a thing possible?'

Next to him, standing at the open door of the boxcar, trying to escape the fetid animal stink, Flipper was so shocked by the sight that he slapped his metal claw against the woodwork, wrenching out wood splinters as he did so.

'Great buckets of flying shit, One Ball, you're right. Man, I don't believe the evidence of my glassy orbits. I swear I don't.' He shook his greying head in a gesture of total disbelief.

Squatting in the dirty straw next to the boxcar's glowing pot-bellied stove, Sergeant Schulze stopped turfing black dirt from beneath his toenails with his bayonet and snapped at Corporal Matz, his long-suffering running mate, 'All right, you little Bavarian barnshitter. Don't just sit there with yer pants down playing with yersen. Go and see what those two Christmas tree soldiers are making all the racket about.'

'Why me?' Matz answered like a man sorely tried. 'And I'm not playing with mesen. I'm trying to get my wooden leg on. We're there.'

'Why?' the big red-faced sergeant snorted. ''Cos rank hath privileges and as a sergeant, I've got more privileges than you, you little aspagarus Tarzan. Now haul yer arse over there and see what's going on.'

Matz mumbled something and Schulze said, without actually having heard him, 'I can't shove it up there. I've got a

24

double-decker bus up there already.' He guffawed coarsely at what he thought was his great sense of humour. Matz pushed his way through the crowd of unshaven, unwashed SS veterans, some of them hunting for lice in the seams of their shirts, others looking for anything they could sell on the local black market in order to buy 'booze and beaver'. Thrusting Flipper out the way, the little one-legged corporal peered out at the platform as the troop train finally came to a stop.

He gasped. Caught completely off guard by the sight on the platform, he cried, head raised as if appealing to some god on high. '*Grosser Gott!* It's not possible. No, in three devils' name, it ain't. I just can't believe it!'

'Believe what?' Schulze bellowed.

Next to Matz, One Ball winced and his hands flew to his abdomen to cap his injured testicles. 'Not so loud, Sergeant Schulze,' he pleaded. 'When you shout like that, you set my remaining testicle off tingling.'

'In half a mo, my dicebeaker –' Schulze meant his big jackboot – 'will set yer yeller arse off tingling if you don't hold yer water,' Schulze growled threateningly, as he rose to his feet. 'Now what's frigging well going on?' he demanded.

Matz hesitated, as if he couldn't bring himself to say what he was now looking at, his little, yellow monkey face set in an expression of total, absolute shock. 'There's a young SS man over there on the . . .' His voice faltered as if he couldn't bring himself to state what he had seen.

'Go on, arse-with-ears,' Schulze urged.

'. . . platform and . . . he's drinking milk!'

Schulze gasped sharply, as if he had just been punched in the guts, hard. 'Did you say *milk*?!'

Matz nodded, as if he didn't trust himself to say more.

'An SS man drinking milk?'

Again Matz nodded.

Schulze hesitated no longer. He pushed his way through

the crowd and halted at the open door. For a moment his vision was clouded by the steam rising from the locomotive, as the driver applied his brakes and the great metal wheels gave one final clatter. Then he saw the SS man – boy would have been a better word.

He was standing there, cap with its silver skull-and-crossbones pushed to the back of his cropped blond hair, his rifle slung carelessly over his skinny right shoulder, raising a canteen of frothy white milk to his lips – there was no doubt about it. It was definitely milk.

Schulze tugged hastily at his collar, as if he were being strangled and couldn't get enough air. His face turned a brick red and his eyes seemed to bulge from his head. A blue vein started to tick electrically at the side of his cheek. 'Milk!' he gasped.

'There's another of 'em over there,' Matz said urgently. 'And he's drinking milk as well.'

'But SS men don't drink milk,' Schulze objected in a voice that he hardly recognized as his own. 'SS men drink suds . . . they drink firewater . . . They've even been known to drink hair oil, anything that contains alcohol. But milk . . .' His voice faltered away, as if he didn't understand the world anymore.

'Perhaps they aren't real SS,' Matz suggested in an awed voice. 'Perhaps it's some Frog trick on us honest Germans. I mean you can't trust folk who make love with their lips, can yer.'

'Oh, yes, they are real SS,' Flipper said, raising his wooden arm. 'Look at that one over there. You can see his arm title.' He squinted hard and tried to make out what the black-and-silver band around the young soldier's sleeve read. Finally he had it. 'Sarge, it's the Hitler Youth Division . . . The Führer's fucking babies.'

Schulze clapped his big hand to his head in a gesture of absolute despair.

'Heaven, arse and cloudburst!' he exclaimed weakly. 'So

that's where we are. Comrades, let's face it. We've really landed in the shit right up to our hooters.'

Next to him Matz crossed himself hastily and said, 'God help us all. Now we're really for it.'

Outside, the young SS men of the Black Guards' newest division drank their milk greedily like overgrown babes sucking fervently at their mother's breast . . .

Further up the train in their relatively comfortable compartment, von Dodenburg stared out at the crowded platform of Caen station. They'd seen scenes like this a dozen times since the war had started in what seemed now another age. Little boys in short pants, rattling their collection cans, collecting for the 'Winter Relief'. Whores standing in the shadows offering their wares in soft, frightened voices. 'Chained dogs', hard-faced military policemen with the silver gorget of their office hanging around their necks, patrolling in pairs, eyeing every soldier suspiciously, as if he were a potential deserter. Sobbing girlfriends hanging round the necks of their soldier friends, as if it would take the 'chained dogs' to tear them apart. And here and there, comfortably fat middle-aged civilians in ankle-length leather coats, which creaked as they moved through the throng. They had Gestapo written all over them.

Von Dodenburg sighed and turned to Pill, who was watching the scene with him. 'Penny for them, Pill?' he said softly.

The middle-aged surgeon to the Assault Regiment SS Wotan shrugged carelessly. 'Don't think my thoughts are worth that much, Kuno. You and I have seen it all before . . . Too often.' He emphasized the two words, suddenly angry. 'Look at those kids drinking their milk. They're next.'

Von Dodenburg didn't need to ask 'next for what?'. He knew what their fate was going to be.

'Hitler Youth – naturally *they*'ll be full of piss and vinegar. But they're only wet-nosed kids, who should be home with their mothers, instead of—' He paused. One of the leather-coated Gestapo men was looking up at them, a cynical look on his coarse, broad face as he chewed an unlit cigar from one side of his thick-lipped mouth to the other.

Instinctively von Dodenburg nodded his approval. Even members of the SS's most elite regiment had to be careful with the Gestapo. They knew no mercy.

The Gestapo man, recognizing the two SS officers' rank, gave them a kind of salute, though there was nothing respectful about it, and passed on through the throng, which parted fearfully in front of him.

'What do you think this sudden change of posting means for us, Kuno?' Pill asked as the Gestapo tough disappeared. 'I mean, what's left of Wotan needs a good deal of rest and recuperation after what the boys have been through on the Leningrad front. My guess is that only half of the survivors are really fit for frontline duty immediately, if that's what we're here for, Kuno.'

Von Dodenburg's harshly arrogant face broke into a worried frown. 'Don't remind me, Pill. All I know is that we received the change of order at Father Christmas's brothel from Reichsführer SS Himmler personally. The signal stated that the change had the personal and immediate approval of our Führer.'

Pill wasn't impressed by the big names. He persisted yet again with, 'Why? Why should we be sent here, a bunch of broken-down old stubble-hoppers, who need a month's rest back home with mother before they should be allowed even near a rifle or machine gun again?'

By way of an answer, von Dodenburg nodded at the window. 'If anyone can tell us that, my dear old pill-pusher, it's that particularly obnoxious gentleman now bearing down upon us in full, self-important haste.' He laughed cynically, as Pill turned to stare at the newcomer striding masterfully down the platform towards their coach.

'Great crap on the Christmas tree!' Pill exclaimed. '*Him!*'

In the same moment that von Dodenburg spotted the Hitler Youth Division's new political officer, Schulze did too. He gave Matz a savage dig in his skinny ribs and snorted, 'Willyer get a load of that, Matzi.'

Catching himself just in time from falling, an angry curse died on the little money-faced corporal's lips as he saw who it was. 'The Creeper!' he exclaimed. 'That frigging arse-kissing bastard. And he's still wearing rubber-soled boots so that he can creep up on some poor unsuspecting stubble-hopper and take his frigging name. I thought that bastard had snuffed it years ago.'

But for the moment Schulze wasn't listening. His hatred of the weasel-faced officer with his pince-nez in imitation of their superior Reichsführer SS Himmler was too great. He hawked loudly. Next instant he had spat a great wad of green-coloured phlegm out of the door to land just in front of those highly polished rubber-soled boots which had given the 'Creeper' his name back in Italy the year before.

The Creeper jumped back hastily, as if he had just been stung. He glared at the big, tough NCO. Angrily he cried, *'Du Dreckschwein.* Couldn't you see I was coming?'

Schulze turned his head to one side and cocked his hand to his big ear, as if he were deaf. 'What, sir?' he quavered. 'I didn't quite hear.'

The Creeper's pale face flushed an even deeper red. 'I said, couldn't you see me?'

Schulze shrugged his shoulders, as if it was impossible for him to understand, while Matz tugged at the straps of his wooden leg and Flipper slapped his artificial arm against the woodwork.

'God in heaven!' the officer cried. 'What kind of mad-house is this?'

Meekly One Ball piped up with, 'SS Assault Regiment Wotan, sir. All that's left of us. We're all cripples really. Most of us are like this as well.' He tapped the side of his head with a significant wink at the enraged officer. 'Not got all their cups in the cupboard. Crazy as loons.'

The Creeper trembled violently. He clenched his puny fists

together as if he were only controlling himself by a sheer effort of naked willpower, for he already realized that he was being made fun of. Through gritted teeth, he hissed, 'I shall be keeping my eye on you dirty lot, mark my words. You'll be in trouble, serious trouble, if you get on the wrong side of me.'

Hidden deeper in the boxcar someone farted, long, slow and insolently. Someone else laughed. It was too much for the Creeper. He turned and marched off, aware that behind his back a score of more of the 'old hares' were laughing silently at his scarlet-faced discomfiture.

Schulze relaxed. Without taking his eyes off the platform, he said to the man who had farted, 'Fine bit of work there, Heinz. But try next time to drag out the low notes a bit longer. It sounds more insulting. Yes —' he raised his voice and added proudly, 'there ain't many regiments where the men can fart as well as they do in SS Assault Regiment Wotan. If anyone can fart a really good insult it's us, comrades.'

He laughed and they joined in. Opposite, standing next to one of the raddled whores, the pretty French girl in the headscarf laughed too at the way the big *Boche* had made fun of the officer. All the same, she didn't forget to make a mental note of the name of the regiment he had given – SS Assault Regiment Wotan. London would be glad of that kind of information.

Five

A little contemptuously, Sergeant Schulze looked around at the circle of eager, young, unspoiled faces of his new squad of the 'Baby Division'. Outside on the parade ground, NCOs barked commands, officers, self-important, holding clipboards, strode back and forth and in the distance there was the metallic clatter of tracks as the new division's armour set off on another afternoon exercise in the Normandy countryside. Sergeant Schulze, being Sergeant Schulze, naturally, wasn't going to indulge in any strenuous exercise, if he could avoid it, especially as he had eaten a large plate of Sauerkraut and pig knuckle, washed down by several litres of good Munich 'suds' for his midday 'snack'. 'If I move suddenlike, arse with ears,' he'd confided in Corporal Matz, 'that Sauerkraut'll go through me like shit through a goose. *Compris?*' he had added, using his newly acquired command of the French language.

'If the Creeper catches you goofing off,' Matz had warned him darkly, 'he'll have yer by the short arm good and proper.'

'He's got to catch Frau Schulze's handsome son first, ain't he,' Schulze had answered, in no way worried by the danger, and he had belched pleasurably in anticipation of a nice, easy spring afternoon.

Now he addressed his command as they squatted in the back of the empty tank hangar, all eyes on the burly, red-faced NCO, his chest heavy with the medals of four years of campaigning on three continents and in a dozen different

31

countries. He let them wait. Savouring the taste once more, he turfed pieces of Sauerkraut and pig knuckle out of his teeth before nodding to Corporal Matz and commanding, 'All right, Corporal, let's get on with it. There's a war to be won. No time to waste.'

Matz muttered something under his breath and Schulze feigned not to hear his suggestion of a sexual act which he knew was physically impossible. '*Achtung*, you cardboard soldiers. Sit at attention!' The 'Babies', all in their teens and all volunteers for the newest SS division from the Hitler Youth, fervent National Socialists to the man, sat up rigidly.

Matz sniffed, as if he had just smelled something unpleasant below his nostrils. 'Alright,' he said. 'Now me and Sergeant Schulze here are gonna tell you something about real soldiering, not this barrack-square bullshit. We wants yer attention, you lot o' piss-pansies. This ain't yer old five against one.' He made an explicit sexual gesture with his right hand. 'This is real stuff, straight from the horse's mouth.' He looked directly at Sergeant Schulze, who was still sucking his teeth pleasurably. No one laughed. The 'Babies' were far too serious.

Schulze rose ponderously to his feet, towering above the teenage volunteers. 'Survival at the front is what I'm gonna talk about,' he said easily, flashing a glance around their eager young faces and telling himself that if he didn't care for these youthful wet-tails, they'd snuff it in their first battle. They looked to him like another batch of cannon fodder, the kind that had been coming – and going quickly – into the SS for years now. The 'old hares' seemed to have vanished. He sniffed.

'First disease and frigging insects. Up at the front there are insects and creepers of all frigging shapes and sizes. There's mosquitoes that can blow up yer kisser to the size of a football in zero comma nix seconds. Then there's the lice, real felt lice. They're the worst, aren't they, Corporal Matz?'

Matz opened his eyes. 'If you say so, Sarge,' he conceded gloomily. His mind was elsewhere, pondering whether he'd be able to get into Fifi's knickers, as he would have put it in his own dainty manner. The lively, flashing-eyed French girl who was behind the bar in the estaminet outside the barracks looked willing. But with all the randy young soldiers around, Matz knew in advance she wouldn't be cheap. She wouldn't spread them for a salami, or even a carton of 'lung torpedoes'. It'd have to be something more substantial than cigarettes.

Dismissing Matz, Schulze warmed to his subject. 'There's many a time in Russia,' he continued, 'when I've found a hundred, perhaps even two hundred of the little buggers feasting on my alabaster torso.' Schulze blew out his chest imposingly to emphasize his point. 'And remember, felt lice lay eggs twelve times a frigging day. Them eggs survive ten days on one meal of yer blood. That means . . .' He did a quick calculation, while his teenage listeners began to wriggle and scratch as if they were already infected by Sergeant Schulze's celebrated 'felt lice'.

The big NCO changed the subject, warming up to it mightily. 'Then there's the frigging flies. They're almost as bad as the felt lice. Once, in Africa or somewhere, we was stationed next to a cavalry division, wasn't we, Matz?'

Matz came to with a start. He was immersed in a delightful vision of rogering Fifi behind her own bar. She had her skirt thrown up at the back, exposing her delicious rump, wriggling it with pleasure while he was shafting her, going at it like a fiddler's elbow. 'Yes, Sergeant Schulze,' he said, the visions vanishing rapidly, as Schulze continued.

'Now nags crap! Holy Moses, don't they just produce crap! One of their sergeants told me at the time that yer average cavalry division with 6,000 of them crap-legged manure machines produces over forty tons of the stuff a day. So you can imagine the flies. Great big blue things what have a kick like that of a mule and arse as big as a yellow-arsed canary—'

'*Senior Sergeant Schulze!*' The well-known voice cut into the big NCO's lecture on 'real soldiering'. 'What in three devils' name is going on here? You were supposed to be out in the field with your squad, practising close-armed combat?'

Schulze took it all in his stride. He sprang to his feet, every inch the dutiful non-commissioned officer. '*Achtung!*' he cried.

The young men rose as one, coming to the position of attention, while Schulze placed his helmet on his shaven head and adjusted it very carefully.

Quivering with barely suppressed rage, the Creeper cried, 'I asked you a question, Schulze.'

Schulze didn't seem to hear. Instead, he faced the officer, towering above the pale-faced National Socialist Leadership Officer with his sickly face and rubber-soled jackboots, and, staring at some distant object, bellowed at the top of his voice, 'Sergeant Schulze and fifty men reporting, all present and correct, *sir*!' He swung the Creeper a tremendous salute, narrowly missing knocking off the latter's cap so that he had to step back hastily in order to avoid the NCO's hamlike fist.

The Creeper trembled visibly. 'I asked you a question, Schulze.'

'*Yessir.* Why am I not with my squad practising close-armed combat, *sir*? With your permission, *sir*, I shall tell you, *sir*.' Schulze hammered home every 'sir' as if it were a term of insult and the Creeper knew it. His sallow face flushed an angry red.

'I don't want to hear—'

But Schulze didn't give him a chance to protest. Instead he intoned, as if he were giving a lecture: 'The aim of close-armed combat is to render the enemy harmless, using all available weapons. These weapons may range from the expected ones – handguns, bayonets and the like – to the unexpected – a helmet strap, the heel of your boot, even a sliver of ordinary wood plucked from the nearest tree.

Perhaps, *sir*, you will allow me to demonstrate.' He didn't wait for the Creeper's answer. Instead he turned smartly to his running mate and barked, 'Corporal Matz, put on yer helmet and draw your bayonet. *Sir*, I will now demonstrate how to use the helmet strap of the enemy's helmet as a killing weapon even when the enemy is armed with a drawn bayonet.'

'SERGEANT SCHULZE!' the Creeper shrieked.

But still Sergeant Schulze seemed to be too wrapped up in his lecture to hear, and even the fanatical teenage soldiers of the 'Hitler Youth' were beginning to realize that the old hare was sending up the officer and were starting to grin and murmur among themselves. It was too much for the Creeper. He turned and strode away rapidly, slapping that famous notebook, in which he was wont to note the misdeeds of the ordinary soldier, against his thigh in barely concealed agitation . . .

Two kilometres away, von Dodenburg stood on the top of a personnel carrier, observing the mock attack of the panzer battalion through his glasses, while next to him, Standartenführer Witt, the commander of the Hitler Youth Division, beamed, obviously very proud of his 'babies'. 'You can see, von Dodenburg,' he said, lowering his own glasses, 'that young as they are, my boys, they show all the dash of the old SS and plenty of expertise, too. They need only some more battlefield experience and then, I am sure, when the Anglo-Americans come they'll do us proud.'

Witt had been out of combat for nearly two years now while he had prepared to build up this latest SS division. It was obvious that he had forgotten what the real battlefield was like; the tactics of his young soldiers showed it. The formation of Panther tanks now driving forward against enemy dug in on the hills to their front would have been wiped out by now. In particular, they hadn't taken into account that the Western Allies dominated the skies over Europe. In a real attack they would have been here, there and everywhere, blasting all hell out of the Panthers below. Witt looked at von Dodenburg's thin hawklike face as he studied the advancing Panthers. 'You're not convinced, von Dodenburg?' he asked.

Now Kuno lowered his glasses, but he didn't answer the question directly. Instead he asked one of his own. 'What is our overall strategy to be when the Anglo-Americans land, *if* they land here?'

Witt didn't hesitate. Proudly he puffed out his enormous chest and said, 'Our strategy has been worked out by the Führer personally. While the infantry holds the enemy on the landing beaches, we assemble and when the Führer gives the order, we march.' He clenched his fat fist. 'And smash them, von Dodenburg. It will be another Dunkirk.' His eyes glowed fervently.

Von Dodenburg still wasn't convinced. 'So, Standarten-führer, if I understand you correctly, your tanks wait till our infantry holds the enemy on the beaches and as soon as the Führer at his headquarters in the West, perhaps some three or four hundred kilometres from Normandy, gives the order, the division marches.'

'Exactly.'

'But aren't there several imponderables here?'

'Imponderables? How do you mean, von Dodenburg?'

'Well, there is Allied air for one thing. I don't know about the tides here in Normandy. But it is certain that the enemy will commence their invasion in order to give themselves the max. number of daylight hours. So your panzers, when the Führer order comes – and there will he delays naturally between the time of landing and the Führer's decision – they will be advancing in daylight under a sky dominated by the enemy. I fought in Italy last year and I know, Standartenführer, just how devasting Allied air power can be.'

Witt frowned, but said nothing. Over in the fields, the Panthers were lumbering into the attack, while here and there anti-tank gunners, playing the enemy, fired tracer instead of shells at the metal monsters. Von Dodenburg could see the tracer bullets bouncing off their steel hides like glowing golf balls.

'Then, sir, there is the question of airborne troops. I know the enemy has several divisions of paratroops. Allied strategy is usually dull and old-fashioned when compared with ours, but they have learned by now how to use paras. There is nothing to stop them dropping several such airborne divisions between us and the beaches, say on the line of the Caen Canal and the River Dives.'

Witt seized the point eagerly. 'Drive a few kilometres further towards the coast, von Dodenburg, and you will see just how well prepared our anti-air landing preparations are. We've been working on them for several months now. Every open field is criss-crossed by poles bearing mines and attached to one another by stout wire ropes that would tear the wings off an enemy glider attempting to land—'

The sudden high-pitched burr of a machine gun firing altogether drowned the rest of the fat SS general's words. Bullets pattered the length of the personnel carrier like heavy summer raindrops. In front, the driver screamed shrilly and slumped over his wheel, blood pouring from his shattered face. The left track collapsed. Witt went over the side, caught off balance. Von Dodenburg, caught by surprise just like the rest, had just time to see three men running from the nearest m.g. post, and attempt to draw his pistol, when he was struck in his upper right arm. It was a blow like that of a heavy club. He gasped. What felt like a red-hot poker bored into his flesh and he knew from his past battlefield experience that he had been hit. 'God damn it!' he exclaimed bitterly, as whistles started to shrill urgently and officers shouted angry orders, while the Panthers rumbled to a sudden halt. Then von Dodenburg felt himself weakening. The strength seemed to ebb out of his body. His knees gave

way like those of a newborn foal. He slipped to the deck
and then fell heavily over the side of the wrecked personnel
carrier. A moment later everything went black and he knew
no more.

Six

The French nurse who tended von Dodenburg in the Caen hospital was friendly and spoke German. More importantly she was very pretty with a figure so splendid that Schulze, who now stood guard together with Matz on Pill's explicit orders over his CO's room, maintained more than once, 'I'd sacrifice my left ball for a feel of her tits.' And he would smack a wet kiss on the back of his hamlike fist and add, 'A stubble-hopper like yours truly could die happy with his head between them tits.'

But Sergeant Schulze was not fated naturally to have to make the supreme sacrifice for a feel of the French nurse's breasts. She was friendly enough to the two NCO bodyguards but if she had eyes for anyone in particular in the *Boche*, it was the wounded officer, whom she tended lovingly, even bathing his private parts with extra gentle care and with none of the roughness nurses normally reserve for anything to do with a male patient's sexual organs. Not that von Dodenburg particularly liked the way she washed his loins, bathing them with warm water and scented soap that could only have come from the French black market. She was too pretty for that and it was hard, very hard, for him to restrain his sexual desire when she came close and her hand gently took hold of his penis. As Matz confessed to Schulze when he heard of the French nurse's attentions, 'With most of them nurses, you couldn't get a stiff 'un if they tugged at it till Judgement Day, they're so ugly. But with her . . .' He shrugged and looked puzzled. 'Don't know how the CO does it. Perhaps officers and gents are built different from common old ugly stubble-hoppers.' With a sigh, Schulze had been forced to agree. After all he couldn't find any other explanation for the 'old man's' restraint.

Kuno von Dodenburg, however, had other problems on his mind than the attention of the pretty nurse, Yvette Bogex. Now that his shoulder had started to give him less pain and was showing all the signs of healing well, he started to think of the future and the role that what was left of SS Assault Regiment Wotan would have to play in it. He didn't like the Führer's plan one bit, and what would become of his old hares once the plan was put into operation.

For he had guessed that not only would Wotan be expected to stiffen the morale of the 'Baby Division' in its first combat action, but that the powers that be would want his handful of survivors to take over command functions when the Hitler Youth started to suffer casualties, as the teenagers eager for glory would surely do. That would mean his men would have to lead from the front – and those who led from the front were usually the first to die.

The regiment – Wotan! a harsh little voice at the back of his mind would click on at this juncture. Is that all you think about? Isn't there anything else in your life, but Wotan?

In truth there wasn't. Sometimes he would answer that harsh cynical voice aloud, saying, tears of self-pity in his eyes, 'But what else have I left? Family, honour, all gone or about to go. Fatherland? Run by a madman, eating up its own children – those babes out there – like a cannibal. A man has to have something to which he can cling, surely?'

Once, right at the beginning when he was troubled so much by these thoughts in the middle of the night, he must have cried out. In a troubled half-sleep, his sheets wet with sweat, he felt her cool hand on his fevered brow – or thought he did. She appeared to stroke him, whispering in French till he slept. But in the morning she was her usual self, going about her sickroom tasks without any comment. In the end he told himself she must have been a figment of his imagination, self-deception of the nicest kind.

At the beginning of May, when Pill informed him that it wouldn't be long now and that if the medical board agreed, he would be discharged back to the 'Baby Division', the Creeper, or Sturmbannführer Kriecher, to give him his full name and rank, appeared surprisingly in the sickroom. Frowning severely at Sergeant Schulze, who was staring down at the cathedral, Schmeisser machine pistol resting on his knees, as if he were ready at a moment's notice to mow down the peaceful churchgoers below, he ordered, 'You may leave us, Sergeant Schulze. This is confidential. I have something to talk over with Obersturmbannführer von Dodenburg.'

For a moment it looked as if Schulze might refuse the Creeper's order, but von Dodenburg nodded to the giant NCO urgently and he slouched out, muttering to himself. The Creeper waited till he had closed the door behind him before saying hurriedly, 'We've caught one of them. At least the chained dogs have.' He smiled in triumph as if he personally had achieved something.

From the bed von Dodenburg stared up at the Political Officer, puzzled. 'Caught whom?' he echoed.

'One of the French swine who tried to kill you and Standartenführer Witt.'

'Oh, you mean the accident.'

The Creeper looked down at von Dodenburg as if he thought that his wound had affected his mental capacity. 'It wasn't an accident, sir.'

'How do you mean? I know now that those chaps who fired on us deserted, but I assumed they did that because they were afraid of the consequences of their mistake.' He smiled. 'After all, it's not every day that a soldier tries to kill his divisional commander, though I must admit there are some in Russia I would have gladly murdered.'

The Creeper wasn't amused. 'They weren't deserters from the Hitler Youth, sir. They were members of that damned

Maquis of theirs. It was a deliberate attempt to kill the most important senior officers of the Caen area.'

Von Dodenburg whistled softly. 'How do you know?' he asked.

'Because the one we've caught has begun to sing. Commissar Krueger of the local Gestapo always maintains he could make even an Egyptian mummy sing like a yellow canary, to use his own words. Well, he's done so in this case.'

'And . . . ?'

Outside, Yvette Bogex, the French nursing sister, put down her tray with the afternoon coffee, and said to the two old stubble-hoppers, in her delightfully accented German, 'Here you are – coffee. Ersatz.' She shrugged prettily and her breasts went up and down beneath her white apron as if on an express lift.

Schulze's eyes nearly popped out of their sockets. Hastily he dabbed his lips; he was drooling already.

'But there's a little something for you, gentlemen, to liven the acorns up.' She pulled a small flatman of brandy out of her apron pocket and handed it to Matz. He accepted it with a hand that shook badly. 'Calvados would be better, but—' Again she shrugged and those wonderful breasts, the nipples clearly visible under the thin material of the apron, rose and fell. Hastily Schulze tugged at his collar, his face beetroot red as if the collar had abruptly become too tight for him, and he was being strangled.

'Thank you, Nurse,' Schulze said in a voice that he hardly recognized as his own. 'You are very gracious.'

Matz looked up at his running mate in amazement. He'd never heard Schulze talk like that before. *You are very gracious!* Christ on a crutch, Schulze would be drinking his coffee with his little pinky extended outwards next. Before you'd know it, the big bugger'd be turning into a 'warm brother'.

'I wonder why that other officer is so excited?' the French nurse asked casually.

Schulze was too overcome by her presence and the close proximity of those wonderful breasts, which seemed about to

42

break loose from their confines at any minute – something he swore he'd give his left testicle to see – to answer. Matz, however, did it for him. 'The officer thinks they've caught the bastard who tried to shoot our CO,' he explained. 'The talk is that they're going to put the bastard against a brick wall and shoot him – toot sweet.' He aired his new-found French with a flourish.

Her dainty white hand flew to her mouth as if in alarm. 'But who would want to shoot Obersturmbannführer von Dodenburg?' she asked. 'He is such a fine fellow.'

Now it was Matz's turn to shrug. 'Don't ask me, *m'selle,*' he answered. We live in a strange, rotten world. Everybody's shooting everybody these days, it seems.' And with that pro-found statement he nudged a still awestruck Schulze, saying, 'All right, arse-with-ears. Come out of your trance. I'm off. You're in charge now.' And with that he was gone. It was only when he was outside in the busy cobbled streets of the old cathedral city that it struck him that Nurse Bogex seemed to be a little bit too interested in the goings-on of Witt's 'Baby Division'. He wondered why for a moment. Then he saw Fifi, standing at the door of the estaminet, cigarette stuck in the corner of her scarlet lips, busily engaged in pulling up her black stocking, twisting a knot to hold it up around her plump white thigh and in an instant he had forgotten all about Nurse Bogex's strange interest in the 'Babies' . . .

Up in his room, the Creeper was finishing his conversation with von Dodenburg. Indeed it had been more of a lecture than a conversation. The pasty-faced, bespectacled officer, who had been a schoolteacher in civilian life and talked like one when he was given half a chance, had explained that the Abwehr* had become concerned about the activities of the local French resistance in recent months. For over three years ever since the German Army had occupied Normandy, there had been little trouble with the locals. The factory workers

*The German Secret Service. *Transl.*

had been happy with the way that the German authorities had ensured there had been full employment for them in the war industries. The farmers, too, had mellowed, motivated as they were mostly by greed and a distrust of the central authority in faraway Paris. The Germans had severed their connection with Paris and had guaranteed a market for their produce with the local German army units. There had been no reason for most of them to want to fight the occupiers in the deadly war in the shadows.

'Now,' the Creeper had pontificated, 'the dastardly English in their usual manner are buying allies with those damned Horsemen of St George of theirs.' He meant sovereigns, which bore the emblem of England's patron saint as a horseman slaying the dragon. 'They are hiring the thugs, the degenerates, the ne'er-do-wells to do their dirty business for them. Spying, sabotage, stabbing our innocent young boys in the back in the most treacherous manner—'

Here, von Dodenburg had held up his good arm for silence. As the Creeper stopped, von Dodenburg said, 'I understand. But that is the kind of war that has been going on behind the front in Russia for years now. Patriots or rogues, it doesn't matter who these French people are, they are doing the work of the enemy and we haven't been able to stop them, whatever their motives. Even if they are only in the minority they can coerce the majority into working with them. They have their ways of doing so.'

'But we *can* stop them,' the Creeper leapt in eagerly, as von Dodenburg paused for breath, his wounded arm beginning to ache once more. 'We *must* stop them before the rot sets in on a larger scale, as it did in Russia.'

'How?'

'A public execution here in Caen, in front of the cathedral if you like. It would be a significant warning to the others. It would show them that the iron hand of New Germany crushes all that stands in our way.'

If von Dodenburg had been in a better mood he would have

laughed at the Creeper's antiquated bombast. But he wasn't in a good mood. Instead he snapped angrily, 'Bullshit, and you know it, Sturmbannführer. Hang them or shoot them down there and all you'll create is martyrs.'

The Creeper flushed a deep red, but he didn't respond. He knew that von Dodenburg, the handsome young swine, was a genuine hero, decorated by the Führer himself, admired by Himmler, head of the SS. All the same, the ex-teacher made a mental note of this interchange. It might well be useful one day when he took his revenge, which he surely would. 'Sir,' he said, lowering his gaze so that von Dodenburg couldn't see the anger in his gaze behind the pince-nez he affected, 'it is out of my hands, now. There will be a public execution of the swine we caught. On orders from Standartenführer Witt personally! The French authorities have been ordered to attend and arrangements are being made for the general public as well.'

'I should imagine they'll be rushing to see the execution of one of their fellow Frenchmen,' von Dodenburg sneered.

The Creeper ignored the remark, though again he noted it. 'Now, sir, the reason I have come to see you in your sickroom today.'

'Go on. I'm all ears, Sturmbannführer.'

'Standartenführer Witt wants no slip-up. He knows his men—'

'*Boys.*'

'Rightly, boys, as you say, sir, and boys might well make a mess of an execution. A firing squad is a tricky business.'

Von Dodenburg stared hard at the Creeper, suddenly aware he was going to be involved in something he didn't particularly like.

He was right.

'Your men, sir, are all old hares. I know they are ill-disciplined. All the same, they will not worry when called upon to shoot a man who has tried to kill their CO as Standartenführer Witt's boys would—'

'You mean, you want me to form a firing squad out of my men?'

'*Genau.*'

'Because my soldiers, ill-disciplined as they are, wouldn't worry about shooting a fellow human being, even if he's the enemy, in cold blood?'

'Yessir,' the Creeper said stolidly.

Von Dodenburg realized that irony was wasted on the other officer. A vein started to tick angrily at the side of his head. Didn't the prissy ex-schoolteacher understand what his men had been through in Russia to make them the way they were? If they were brutalized and cynical, it had been the war, fighting for their Fatherland, which had brutalized them. They had seen their comrades killed by the dozen, the score, the hundreds. How could they remain innocent and sensitive after that? He opened his mouth to bellow at the Creeper, but he didn't get the chance to do so. There was a soft knock on the door and even before he could call 'Enter', Nurse Bogex opened the door, pushing her trolley piled with medicines and dressings. 'Time to change your dressing, Obersturmbannführer,' she announced cheerfully. 'Have to do it now, gentlemen. The *Stabsarzt* is already doing his rounds and he's a real tartar if we upset his routine.'

Von Dodenburg relaxed. He even smiled at the thought of Pill, the new staff doctor, being regarded as a 'tartar'. He looked up at the Creeper, who sniffed at Nurse Bogex as if the fact that she was French was distasteful to him. 'When?' he asked.

'Day after tomorrow, sir. Zero eleven hundred hours, sir. In the main square opposite the Château and the church of Saint Pierre.'

Von Dodenburg nodded. He had had enough of the Creeper for one day.

The latter took the hint. He clicked his heels together smartly and, turning, went out, shoulders squared, as if he were on the parade ground.

Von Dodenburg smiled at Nurse Bogex. She smiled back, though her dark eyes remained wary. She said, 'Well, General –' the 'General' was a joke between the two of them – 'shall we have a look at our wounds?'

Von Dodenburg said, 'Please.' Then, as she came closer with the surgical scissors, his nostrils were assailed by that delightful fragance she used, totally different from the stink of carbolic he had usually associated with nurses every time he had been in hospital to have his wounds attended to previously. Suddenly he felt almost happy.

Seven

It was cold for spring. A chill wind blew through the grey cobbled alleys of the old town of Caen. In the trees outside the Château, the rooks cawed hoarsely in the still, skeletal branches, as if in protest. But in the waiting crowd of shivering, foot-stamping civilians, all was silence. It was as if the people who had been ordered to watch the public execution of the Resistance man didn't think it quite right to talk. All eyes were fixed on the stake and the backboard which the Germans had erected overnight, so that it had been there when the first farmers had come into town to sell their wares at the great open market.

But if the civilians were silent and subdued, the Germans were in no way inhibited by the solemn event that was to take place here in the square this chill spring morning. The sentries marched back and forth, their young faces hard and alert, as busy staff officers strode across the square, making their preparations, chatting loudly to one another, as if it was right and proper that a man was going to die here soon. Here and there too, other members of the 'Baby Division' in their white fatigues were hammering and sawing, preparing to erect the crooked cross of Nazi Germany on all sides of the square to impress upon these cowed civilians that they, the SS, were the masters not only of Normandy but the rest of Western Europe with power of life and death over the French.

Resting against the stanchion of the review platform, his wounded arm in a sling, his overcoat draped personally by Nurse Bogex over his shoulders, Kuno von Dodenburg viewed the scene in the square with distaste. He had seen this sort of thing often enough before. Back in 1941 when the Russian partisans had first made their appearance behind the front in Russia, murdering lone German soldiers in their beds with their whores, massacring them in lone outposts, he had approved of reprisals. He had thought it had been the best way to bring home to the peaceful members of the occupied Russian community that any attack on the German military would be punished severely. But it hadn't worked. The attacks and the reprisals had escalated so that, in the end, no one had felt safe behind the front, and the German occupiers had been forced to withdraw frontline troops to take on the partisans in what, by 1943, had amounted to regular pitched battles, using air and artillery.

Von Dodenburg frowned and wished he could have a stiff drink. Below, machine pistol cradled in his brawny arms, always at the ready to protect his CO, that rogue Schulze's back pocket bulged with his flatman. He'd obviously come prepared. Very soon he'd slip behind the rostrum and 'pour one down past his collar stud', as he would phrase it. Von Dodenburg's frown changed to a slight wintry smile. Thank God, the SS still had soldiers like Schulze: they were the salt of the earth.

Pill pushed his way through the crowd of self-important divisional staff officers on the platform. 'Someone who looks happy at least,' he said.

'*Guten Morgen, Herr Stabsarzt,*' von Dodenburg joked and bowed slightly in greeting his old friend and regimental surgeon.

Now it was Pill's turn to smile. 'Come off it, Kuno. Staff doctor – me! You know I'm just a broken-down old sawbones, who needs a couple of stiff belts of booze in the morning to stop his hands trembling. And I must admit –' his smile vanished – 'I've had a couple of the same this morning. I don't like this sort of business – don't like it one little bit.'

Somewhere a clock chimed. The two of them stopped their conversation automatically. Silently they counted the strokes. Eleven. In thirty minutes or so it would be all over. As the chimes ended, the big Horch truck drove slowly into the square. There was a gasp from the crowd. They recognized the firing squad immediately. All old hares from Wotan, they sat facing inwards, rifles between their legs, faces set and grim. Veterans that they were, they didn't like this nasty business at all. Von Dodenburg didn't need a crystal ball to tell that. Even that other rogue Corporal Matz looked subdued, the usual lecherous smirk vanished from his wrinkled monkey face. He didn't flash his customary grin at his old running mate Schulze when the truck passed. It was as if he was in another world, cut off from what was taking place here.

The Creeper strode importantly across the square. Today he was wearing his normal boots. Pill and Kuno could hear the stamp of the nails on the cobbles. He was even carrying the honour dirk of the Armed SS. Von Dodenburg told himself that the arsehole was really enjoying this. Now he wished even more fervently that he could swallow a stiff drink, maybe two. But that was out of the question. For now Standartenführer Witt, accompanied by his chief of staff, clever Obersturmbannführer Meyer, were ascending the steps of the rostrum, followed by the local *Prefect* and French Chief of Police. All of them looked grim and, in the case of the two Frenchmen, resigned. It wouldn't be long now.

The minutes passed leadenly. The crowd started to shuffle their feet. Over at the church the clock struck the quarter, As one, those who had watches looked at them, including von Dodenburg. Idly he wondered why he did so. He already knew the time and that there were fifteen short minutes left before they shot the Frenchman. A long way off there came the drone of aircraft. But no one looked up. Everyone was transfixed by the sight of the open truck bearing the victim, wearing a fresh white shirt and with his hands tied behind his back, as it came slowly into the square.

Next to von Dodenburg, Pill whispered, 'It must have been like this during the French Revolution. Another *aristo* being brought to the guillotine.'

Von Dodenburg didn't answer. He wouldn't. His whole attention was concentrated on the young Frenchman, his face a deadly white under his shock of black hair. The youngster had only minutes left to live. Von Dodenburg wondered what was going through his head at this moment. In battle a man didn't have time to consider his fate; his blood was roused, the adrenalin would be pumping and he would be totally concerned with trying to preserve his existence. To be tied to a post, wait till the ceremonials were completed and then to tense for that final blow which would cut off life for ever was an entirely different matter. Veteran of four years of combat that he was, Kuno wondered if he would be able to stand the strain.

Now the prisoner was being led to the stake. He was dragging his feet a little. Otherwise he was composed and repeating the solemn litany read out by the priest from his breviary. Behind them the Creeper, in charge of the firing squad, grasping his dirk, looked on contemptuously. Non-believer that he now was, he probably thought the prayers a lot of Papist mumbo-jumbo. In front of the stake, the victim bent on one knee to receive the priest's final blessing. The drone of engines was getting closer.

The priest stepped back. Still he prayed. The victim waited. Swiftly two NCOs appeared from behind. They seized him and strapped him to the stake and the backboard which would hold him upright in case he fainted before the order to fire was given.

Now the Creeper stamped to attention in front of the prisoner. He held up a blindfold. The French youth shook his head. Von Dodenburg could see he was fighting back his tears. 'God in heaven,' Pill whispered to Kuno, 'this is awful.' Von Dodenburg didn't answer; he couldn't. The Creeper said something. One of the two NCOs who had

51

bound the prisoner to the stake produced a white paper heart. Clumsily he pinned it above the spot where the real organ was located. He stepped back quickly. It was almost there now. The noise of the aircraft was coming in from the west, getting louder by the instant.

The president of the tribunal which had sentenced the youth to death marched towards the bound man. He was an officer from a *Wehrmacht* unit, probably cavalry, for he trailed a long cavalry sabre behind him absurdly. The scabbard clattered on the cobbles. He cleared his throat and then read out the sentence of death. It was obvious that he dared not look the prisoner in front of him directly in the eye.

His piece said, the officer turned and marched off more quickly than he'd approached. Now it was the Creeper's turn to take centre stage, and a contemptuous von Dodenburg could see that the political officer was going to enjoy every minute of it. After all, he was carrying out the execution in front of the *Prominenz*, including the divisional commander. Why, the pasty-faced ex-schoolteacher was probably thinking, perhaps even Reichsführer SS Himmler might hear of my performance.

Now the Creeper turned to the squad of Wotan's old hares. 'Squad,' he barked in his thin voice, his breath fogging on the cold air, 'port arms!'

The veterans could have done a better job of presenting their rifles. But their hearts weren't in the job and they performed sloppily. Not that their CO von Dodenburg cared. He felt like they did: this execution should not be taking place.

The Creeper waited, then he cried, '*Leg an!* Clumsily the firing squad raised their rifles to their shoulders and the firing position. The Creeper drew the business out. Obviously, when now every eye was upon him, he was going to make the most of his moments of glory. He let the firing squad wait. Slowly he started to raise his dirk to shoulder height. At the stake the young Frenchman wet himself with fear. Pill bit his bottom lip. He could see the wet stain growing larger on the poor man's shabby trousers. 'Damned shit!' he cursed to von Dodenburg. 'Kuno, the poor swine's gone and pissed himself.'

Kuno didn't reply. He could see that. He could also see that the victim was trying to be brave despite the fact that his death was imminent. He braced his shoulders and flung back his head in a gesture of defiance. The Creeper didn't even bother to look at him. Instead he cried in his shrill schoolmaster's voice, as he raised his dirk even higher, not heeding the roar of the aeroplane engines. '*Feu—*'

He never finished the command to fire. In that same instant, the Spitfire dropped out of the low cloud and came hurtling down the approach road to the square at zero feet, the howl of its engines going all out, echoing and re-echoing in the stone chasm. In a flash all was chaos. Old hares that they were, the firing squad broke ranks and dived for cover. At the stake, the Frenchman's head fell forward. He had fainted. Like a giant metal hawk, the Spitfire swept across the square, dragging its shadow behind as the crowd scattered in panic, fighting, gouging, kicking in their haste to get away from what surely would soon come.

It did. The British pilot slowed the plane by lowering his flaps and undercarriage. It was a daring manoeuvre. Any German fighter could have easily shot down the Spitfire, flying as it was now at just over stalling speed. Crouched next to Pill, as here and there the young soldiers of the 'Baby Division' raised their rifles and started firing at the enemy plane, von Dodenburg wondered what the Tommy was going to do and if this sudden appearance over the old city of Caen had anything to do with the Frenchman's execution.

But the pilot didn't give him much chance to consider these questions. Now he swept round in a very tight turn, trailing smoke behind him and, with his undercarriage and flaps still down, came in for the kill. Abruptly the eight machine guns lining the Spitfire's wings crackled into blue-red action. Tracer streamed from the Brownings. Abruptly slugs were hissing through the air all around the *Prominenz*'s rostrum. Wood splintered. The crooked cross flags snapped and fell down. A support gave. The rostrum slipped to one side. Chairs flew everywhere. The mayor yelped with pain. Now they were taking casualties as they lay there in a huddled, confused mass with the Spitfire pilot, clearly visible behind his perspex windscreen, spraying them with bullets.

The attack seemed to last for an age. In reality it was over in a matter of seconds, as the pilot hastily withdrew his undercarriage and soared upwards to a triumphant victory roll above their heads in the same instant that the ancient Citroën came dashing down into the square, men hanging on grimly to its sides as they balanced on the running board, British Sten guns blazing. Even Schulze, old hare that he was, was too startled to react. First the surprise appearance of the Tommy plane, then this car charging straight for where the firing squad lay on the ground, the only one erect in the centre of the square the prisoner. Then he had it. 'Great buckets o' flying crap!' he cried, red-faced with anger. He raised his Schmeisser and started blazing away wildly.

But the men in the car seemed to bear a charmed life. With a squeal of tortured rubber, the Citroën shuddered to a stop. Instantly the men on the running boards dropped to the ground and blazed away at the sentries and the bullet-riddled, shattered podium. One of them ran to the stake. A knife flashed. In an instant the prisoner's bonds were slashed. He staggered, and would have fallen if they had not supported him. Swiftly they dragged him to the car. With another squeal of protesting rubber, the driver swung the long black car round. Its windscreen shattered as one of Schulze's slugs hit it. The driver slammed at the glittering spider's web of broken glass with a hammer. It fell outwards in a rain of shards. He thrust his elbow and cleared a large hole. Then he was off again, reversing and turning in a wild fury as Schulze fumbled, cursing madly, to fit another magazine into the base of the machine pistol.

The driver of the escape car didn't give him a chance to do so. He hit the accelerator. The Citroën shot forward. On the shattered rostrum, a red-faced Standartenführer Witt bellowed at the top of his voice. Stop that damned car NOW! . . . Seven days' leave in Paris for any man who stops it!'

But there was going to be no '*Ooh, la, la*' in 'Gay Paree' for any of Witt's 'Baby Division' that spring. The eager young boys were out of luck. The rescue had been too well planned in London. As the Citroën howled round the corner on two wheels and spurted out of sight, its engine racing frantically, the first of the smoke grenades from the tall eighteenth-century buildings which fringed the street started to explode at the corner. Almost immediately the corner was obscured by choking, blinding, thick smoke. The pursuers came to a sudden halt, reeling back, coughing, spluttering and blinded, their efforts to stop the getaway car stymied even before they had started. In a blind rage, Witt, unable to do anything else, fired his pistol into the sky.

Von Dodenburg shook his head and dismissed the matter. There was nothing he could do. He coughed and fumbled in the wreckage of the shattered rostrum. 'Pill!' he called huskily. There was no answer. Then he saw the familiar gaiters and old-fashioned boots that Pill wore, the same he had worn as a young infantry officer in the trenches. '*Pill!*' he cried. Frantically he clawed at the debris lying on top of the old man. He pulled off the crooked cross flag that Pill had hated so much in these last years, to reveal his friend. A bullet had made a clean, neat red hole in his forehead. Even as he bent to listen for any sign of life, von Dodenburg knew it was too late. The shot had killed the doctor with finesse.

Now he lay there peacefully, the wrinkles smoothed from his kindly old face in death. He might well have been sleeping. But von Dodenburg knew that this was the eternal sleep, the sleep of death. Sadly he pulled down the eyelids, one after the other. Then taking two five-mark pieces from his pocket, he placed them over the unseeing eyes. Another of his old hares had gone. As he rose, not hearing the excited cries, the angry orders, the moans all around him, and clambered down the debris, he wondered how many of them would be left when what surely would start soon commenced . . .

BOOK TWO

Double Treachery

They were men rudely torn away
from the joys of life. Like any other
men whom you take in the mass,
they were ignorant and of narrow
outlook, full of sound commonsense,
disposed to be led and do as they
were bid, enduring under hardships,
long suffering . . . but at intervals
there were cries and dark shudders
of humanity that issued from the
silence and the shadows of their great
human hearts.

Henri Barbusse

One

V on Dodenburg arrived at Berlin's Lehrter Station on May 1st, 1944. But this particular May Day was not celebrated as of old. The happy drunks had long since vanished, as had the fanatical Party faithful. Now the great central station was full of troops and shabby civilians, its glass all blown out by the repeated Allied 'terror raids', with trains from the front arriving at hourly intervals, the loudspeakers booming with foreign names that had long become familiar to the long-suffering civilians waiting for their loved ones; and the little children waving their paper swastika flags handed to them by the stem-looking, cropped-hair Hitler Youth in their short black pants.

For a moment or two, von Dodenburg looked around, a little bewildered by the noise, the emotions of the womenfolk greeting their men from the front, the wailing of the kids, the constant announcements echoing and re-echoing metallically in the bomb-shattered hall.

He had half-expected someone to meet him; after all, this surprise summons to the capital had come from the top, the Tirpitzufer, in the centre of the government complex. But there was no one there. In the end, he walked outside into the morning, the air still smelling of smoke and high explosive from the previous night's RAF bombing attack. Again he paused and looked around.

Berlin and its citizens seemed shabbier than ever. Under-nourished men and painted women, shoulders bent, heads buried in their upturned collars against the stink, hurried through the smoking ruins around the station to their jobs. Ancient wood-burning trucks trundled through the debris-littered streets, packed shoulder to shoulder with earnest-looking middle-aged businessmen, clutching their battered briefcases, which probably contained nothing more than their sandwiches. Here and there among the civilians were the wounded in their striped hospital pyjama uniform. They hobbled about on their crutches. Others were cased in an extended splint which they called the '*Stuka*' because it resembled the gull-like wing of the antiquated dive-bomber. A few were blind, tapping their way hesitantly through the piles of rubble, with black-dotted armbands on their sleeves to warn oncomers of their condition.

Not that anyone worried or cared anymore. The civilians had seen too many horrors already. What were a few pathetic blind young men more or less?

An old woman in ill-fitting man's slacks, carefully gathering cigarette ends thrown away by the soldiers from the gutter, saw him standing there a little hopelessly. She straightened up and pointed to the sign put up on a bombed house after last night's raid. It read: 'WE THANK THEE, O FÜHRER.' She winked and croaked in a thick drinker's voice, 'That we do, don't we, sir? We thank him greatly for all this.' Again she winked.

As a colonel in the SS, clearly identified as such by his black uniform, he thought the old woman was remarkably bold to talk to him like that. But perhaps she was mad, risking being turned in for such defeatist statements. He told himself, it really didn't matter. He said, 'Listen, granny, I want to get to the Tirpitzufer. I don't want to walk. Where do I find a taxi?' He took out a small pack of Juno cigarettes and handed it to her.

She smiled, showing a mouthful of rotten teeth. 'Tailor-made, ain't seen the like of them this many a day.' Hastily she tucked the five cigarettes away somewhere in the depths of her dirty blouse. 'A German woman neither smokes nor paints her face': she repeated the old Party phrase for some reason or other.

'*A taxi.*'

'*Jawohl, Herr General,*' the old woman chortled, clicking to a semblance of attention and saluting von Dodenburg. Now Kuno thought she was really mad, or just plain drunk. All the same she knew where to find a taxi. A few moments later he was walking to 'Parteilokal Fünf', a Party meeting place where, she had assured him, the 'golden pheasants' – she meant the Nazi Party officials called thus on account of the amount of gold braid they wore on their brown Party uniforms – always got what they wanted, including taxis.

The old woman, drunk or whatever she was, was not quite right. Even the 'golden pheasants' were finding it a little difficult to find a taxi in bombed, petrol-ration Berlin that morning, but as the fat Party official, who had put a big glass of Berliner Weisse* into a surprised von Dodenburg's hand, assured him, 'We'll find you one, *Obersturm*. There's nothing we old ones will not do for our boys at the front, especially our own SS.' He laughed so heartily that his fat jowls wobbled and around the table the other Party members nodded hastily. It seemed to a bemused von Dodenburg, finding himself so suddenly surrounded by these fat, middle-aged Party men, who appeared to have done very well for themselves out of the war in comparison to the shabby civilians outside in the streets, that they didn't have the faintest idea of what was going on at the front. Indeed, just a minute before, the fat Party leader had proclaimed, 'Let the Tommies and *Amis* come in the West. We'll give 'em such a sound beating, they'll never come back again. Then these defeatists and traitors in Berlin will have to eat their words. Believe you me, *Obersturm*, the Führer knows what he's about.' Now he crooked his finger at the fat waitress in the too-short dress, 'Trudl, bring us a whisky,

---

*A mixture of beer and lemonade, drunk in Berlin.

a British whisky. The *Obersturm* needs something better than that piss.'

'We're out of British whisky,' the fat waitress replied, easily dodging the fat SA man with the World War medals, who was trying to put his hand up the back of her skirt.

'No English whisky!' Kuno's new friend snorted. 'What are things coming to when hard-working Party officials like ourselves can't get a drink. All right, brandy – a bottle of brandy. And none of that Rhenish muck. Real French brandy. At least the Frogs make a decent drink.'

Von Dodenburg nodded carefully. He wished his taxi would hurry up. He didn't like the Party official and it was hard not to show it. In fact he didn't like any of the brown-shirted Party officials around him with their fake smiles, pot bellies and decorations from the old war. They had gotten rid of their families, having them evacuated to somewhere safe in the country. Now they lived like bachelors again, getting drunk at this time of the morning, obviously trying to replace their fat hausfrau wives with younger models, 'enjoying the war', as they kept stating happily, '– peacetime's going to be terrible.' They had no concept of what was really happening to Germany in this year of 1944, or if they had, they didn't want to accept the dire truth that Germany was going to lose the war.

Von Dodenburg sipped the brandy Trudl had brought – again she had neatly dodged those fat importuning fingers trying to slip up her stocking and to the naked flesh beyond – and told himself he should not be so pessimistic. But he had been like this ever since he had discovered Pill lying dead in the wreckage that morning of the execution and he didn't seem able to shake off his mood. Meeting these self-satisfied golden pheasants had not helped his mood one bit. Indeed the meeting had only depressed him more.

Now his new friend was really getting drunk. He was drinking the strong French cognac out of a mug instead of a normal glass, maintaining that 'back in the trenches just before we went over the top we'd drink this Frog firewater by the bottle. Not that we really needed it. As soon as the Frogs and Tommies saw us coming, they shat their pants right off. Mark my words, it won't be any different when they attempt to land in France soon.'

There were drunken cries of agreement from his Party cronies and suddenly von Dodenburg felt a sense of anger at these self-satisfied brownshirts who would never do the fighting in what was to come and would probably die in their soft beds of old age. 'So, *Kreisleiter*, you think it's going to be that easy?'

'Of course it is,' the other man replied confidently. 'We Germans can outfight the world. We have the men, we have the machines –' he leaned forward suddenly, lowering his voice as he did so – 'and I may tell you, *Obersturm*, we have the surprises the Führer has up his sleeve. His revenge weapons. Now what do you say to that?' he added almost as if he had just won the war personally.

'Not much,' von Dodenburg replied icily.

The *Kreisleiter* looked at him, his fat sweaty face puzzled. 'Did I hear you correctly, *Obersturmbannführer*?'

'You did.'

'Then don't you believe in our German victory?'

'I'm not paid to believe,' von Dodenburg continued in that same icy tone, suddenly hating the fat *Kreisleiter* and everything he stood for. 'I'm paid to fight – *and die* if necessary.'

'You're a queer fish,' the *Kreisleiter* said, while the confident smiles vanished from the fat faces of his cronies.

Von Dodenburg wished the taxi would come and he could get away from this damned place and these awful creeps of Party fanatics.

'But belief is also the basis for any successful combat action,' the *Kreisleiter* said slowly, gazing hard at von Dodenburg. 'You know that as a combat-experienced officer. Or,' he added, 'perhaps you aren't a combat-experienced officer, perhaps not even an SS officer. I've seen one of your kind with all those medals who spoke like you.'

Von Dodenburg shrugged. 'I'm not one bit interested in what you do or don't think. All I'm interested in at the moment is that taxi which will take me to my destination.'

From far away there came the thin wail of the sirens hailing one of the Americans' daily daylight raids on the capital. In that same moment the steady *tick-tock* of the air-defence radio link which was kept running in every public place in the Reich changed to a more urgent *ping-ping*. It was the signal which meant enemy bombers were over German territory and, in this case, heading for Berlin.

Around the *Kreisleiter*, the smiles vanished from the faces of his cronies and one or two of them cocked their heads to one side so that they could hear better. Others downed their drinks hastily, as if they knew they'd soon be running for the cellars. Not the *Kreisleiter*. He was too intent on von Dodenburg and why an SS officer should be so defeatist. 'I can see, *Obersturmbannführer*, that you have little faith in Germany's victory,' he said formally. 'Perhaps it would be better that you showed me your papers and your leave pass. One can't be too careful these days. We are surrounded by spies, traitors and defeatists on all sides—'

'A large formation of enemy terror-bombers are heading in a north-easterly direction.' The harsh official voice drowned the rest of his words. 'They are currently passing the Hanover flak belt. It is believed that they are heading for Berlin . . .'

That did it. The golden pheasants downed their French brandy as one. The *Kreisleiter* did the same, snatched his cap and kicked back his chair. 'We shall talk as soon as this raid is over. You will not leave this place.' Then he was hurrying down the steps to the air-raid shelter with the rest of the suddenly panicked brownshirts, followed by von Dodenburg's cry of 'Victory in 1944'.

Five minutes later von Dodenburg was driving through

the glowing streets, the 'Christmas trees' – great bundles of white, glowing flares – sailing down on both sides, while the flak started to belch smoke and flame, heading for the Tirpitzufer, his mind in turmoil.

Two

K uno von Dodenburg had heard of the master of the Tirpitzufer, situated close to the Führer's own Reich Chancellery Building. All those close to the centre of power in those pre-war years when he had been one of the Führer's up-and-coming SS adjutants had. He had even heard the mysterious officer's nickname. It had been 'Santa Claus'. Why he had never found out. Besides, in the happy, carefree late '30s his mind had been on other things: dances, pretty girls and the possibility of the rapid promotion that a future war might bring. Otherwise, it had seemed to him, he would remain a black-uniformed flunkey, all salutes, clicking heels, and *'Heil Hitler'*, for the rest of his career.

Now, with the bombs thudding to the ground not far off and the flak bellowing, great flashes of angry light slashing the grey sky, here he was about to meet the mysterious spymaster known (behind his back) as 'Santa Claus' at last. Though why he had been summoned from France to meet him – and who in the office of Reichsführer SS Himmler had authorized this meeting – remained a mystery.

The little man in the shabby civilian suit (though he was still a serving admiral) came shuffling down the long corridor, leading two little dogs, and as he came closer a sudden flash of gunfire revealed why he was nicknamed 'Santa Claus'. His look was benign, almost kindly under the shock of unruly snow-white hair. At that moment he looked the most unlikely admiral that von Dodenburg had ever met in his military career. Still, he was aware that

66

this time Father Christmas wouldn't be laying on naughty treats.

As he stopped, Santa Claus hushed the yapping of his dogs and said in a soft, perhaps even slightly sinister voice, 'How good of you to come and see me, Colonel von Dodenburg.' He held out his hand and Kuno took it. The spymaster's grip was soft and slightly damp. It wasn't the grip of a soldier and Kuno felt slightly uneasy with it, especially as Santa Claus seemed to retain his hand longer than was necessary.

'Now then, come along to my office, where we can have a little chat,' Santa Claus said, finally releasing him. 'Let me make you some coffee personally. *Turkish* coffee with real coffee beans and none of that ersatz stuff.'

But if the admiral had something exotic about him, his office was spartan, just a bed, a chair and a desk. There was not even a picture of the Führer on the wall: something very strange for a high official of his type, working only metres from Hitler's new Chancellery. Now as the admiral fussed with his coffee on the little cooker in the corner, the dogs sniffing about his heels as he did so, he said to von Dodenburg, 'I am sure that you are surprised that I called you here. Colonel, eh?' At this juncture he turned and suddenly Kuno felt the power of the man's dark eyes. There was something feline and disquieting about his gaze.

'Yes,' Kuno answered a little lamely. 'It's not often that frontline officers get asked to visit . . . er . . .' He hesitated, wondering what he should call this place.

Santa Claus laughed and said, as he handed Kuno a small cup of turgid-looking coffee, followed by a glass of cold water, 'The spymaster's web, eh?'

'I suppose so, sir,' Kuno answered uneasily. As shabby and as undersized as he was, Santa Claus had a strange, disquieting effect. He looked like a man who knew where the skeletons were buried – and more.

'I shall tell you. But please try the coffee. I pride myself on my coffee and I always serve it when I cook for my staff.'

Cook for my staff! Von Dodenburg could hardly believe his own ears. A German admiral, and one of the most important officials in the Third Reich, cooking for his staff. Was the man, with his shitty dogs, some sort of 'warm brother'?

Santa Claus didn't notice Kuno's puzzled expression, or if he did, he didn't comment on it. Instead he said, 'I thought I'd like to chat with the most experienced SS officer on the front to come in the West. Standartenführer Witt outranks you, but he doesn't have your experience in combat and, besides, you have fought the English twice before in this long war – successfully, too.' He gave Kuno that benevolent smile of his, but the former no longer rose to the bait. There was something about the little spymaster that he didn't quite trust; he had to be on his guard with him.

'Anything I can tell you, sir, I will.'

'Thank you. But first let me tell you a few bits of information that the Abwehr has found out in recent weeks.' He put down his little cup, walked over to the wall, pulled back the curtain to reveal a large-scale map of western France and Britain, covered with a rash of blue and red chinograph marks.

In a completely unprofessional way for a regular officer, Santa Claus tapped the map and said, 'Eastern England. From Portsmouth – *here* – right up to the Humber – *here* – the English, as you know, are preparing to invade France. They will attack in Normandy.'

Von Dodenburg swallowed the hot coffee in a gulp and wished he hadn't – he was that surprised. 'But, sir, we have been informed that the English objective is not really known. There are several possible points of attack.'

'Normandy,' the admiral replied and there was a note of complete certainty in his voice. 'The English, as you know, are a very devious and clever race. They are past masters at deception. Now,' he continued, as if he had settled the matter once and for all, 'we have our eyes on two English divisions in particular, their Sixth Airborne – here in the

Lincolnshire area – and their Third Infantry Division – here to the east of Portsmouth. From their radio traffic, it is clear that they have been working closely together recently. That and certain other evidence we possess makes us believe that the airborne will lead the attack to be followed by the Third in a seaborne assault.' He looked hard at von Dodenburg. 'Now, Colonel, you are much more expert on these matters than I. What would you do with those two divisions if you were this English General Montgomery?'

Kuno was caught off guard by the question, but he reacted swiftly enough. 'I'd do two things. I'd secure the line of the River Dives and the Caen Canal to prevent our Fifteenth Army on the other side of that line from coming to the aid of the Hitler Youth Division, my own formation. At the same time as the airborne troops are landing, I'd rush the seaborne troops of this – er – Third British Infantry Division in the general direction of Caen, using my air force to bomb the Hitler Youth into inactivity.'

'Exactly, young friend,' Santa Claus said hastily. 'Once the Dives–Caen Canal line is sealed off, the only formation of any note which could stop the English follow-up – the Channel Invasion in other words – is your Hitler Youth.' He paused and his little smile vanished. Even the fact that one of the dachshunds was now busy peeing on his right shoe didn't seem to distract him. 'The rest of our formation on that stretch of the coast are third-rate, "stomach battalions", "ear and eyes battalions",* Russians and renegade Tartars, the whole ethnic rabble, mere cannon fodder.'

Von Dodenburg nodded his agreement. That rabble of coastal battalions would be used when the invasion came to stop the enemy for a couple of hours until German formations were ready to counterattack. Then it would be

---

*Men suffering from stomach complaints or problems with their ears and eyes grouped together in battalions for efficiency and con-venience's sake.

up to Witt's 'Baby Division' to deal with the enemy, which, even as inexperienced as they were, the young fanatics could do, especially as they had the advantage of armour and a large number of soldiers for a German division, some twenty thousand men in all. The British infantry had no armour and one of their divisions numbered about 15,000 soldiers.

Santa Claus seemed to be able to read his mind, for he said, 'Even under the circumstances I have just outlined, my dear young friend, your Hitler Youth Division might well be able to stop the enemy's Third Division and effectively delay the English invasion timetable, and remember their English General Montgomery has only a limited number of men. England is scraping the manpower barrel.'

Von Dodenburg nodded his understanding, but at the same time, he still didn't comprehend where this conversation was going. Why was he the recipient of this high-powered intelligence? After all he was merely the commander of a decimated regiment sent to France to bolster up a young SS division commanded by someone else.

Santa Claus enlightened him the next moment. 'Your task in France, I have been informed from certain quarters, is to bolster the fighting ability and morale of Standartenführer Witt's greenhorns. After all, to use your rough soldiers' expression, they are still wet behind the spoons and we all know how boys such as they sometimes crack up in combat.'

Now as the bombs continued to fall and the two dogs became more excited and nervous, the second one began to urinate on the little admiral's shoes. Again he didn't seem to notice; he was so wrapped up in this strange conversation which didn't seem to be leading anywhere in von Dodenburg's opinion.

Santa Claus continued: 'But do you think, my friend, it would be very *wise* to bolster up their courage and keep them fighting, despite heavy losses, until the English advance will have been stalled? Would it be to Germany's advantage?' He looked hard at von Dodenburg.

'*What?*' the latter exclaimed. 'What did you say, sir?'

Frightened by the noise a surprised von Dodenburg made, the second dachshund fled into the corner, trailing urine behind it.

Santa Claus was seemingly not surprised by his reaction. He said, 'I mean this, von Dodenburg. Is it not time for Germany to realize that it is about beaten and that it is time for our poor country to make a decision and gain for itself the best possible terms from the Western Allies?'

Von Dodenburg's reaction was immediate. 'That sounds to me something like treachery, sir.' Yet even as he blurted out the accusation, he remembered his own father, sitting on that worn saddle, swinging his sabre under the flags and portraits of his ancestors who had served Prussia's and Germany's cause loyally and to the bitter end for nearly three hundred years now. Hadn't the old General said the same thing virtually?

'One has to be realistic, young man,' Santa Claus said softly. He waited for the crash of a stick of bombs nearby to end before adding, 'Please pick up my phone.' He indicated the red one on the desk. 'Press the black button, please.'

Shocked and bewildered, von Dodenburg complied automatically. In his heart he knew he should have refused, shouted at the little admiral in the shabby suit that he would report him immediately to the authorities for defeatism, even treachery. Yet he seemed unable to do so; he didn't know why. He pressed the button as ordered. For a moment nothing happened. Then there was a click, as if a recording had started and a voice speaking in a thick Swabian accent followed – and there was no mistaking who the speaker was. Von Dodenburg had heard him speak on the radio and in the newsreel interviews in Africa often enough. He said, 'Comrade, I am loath to make this grave statement but it has to be made, cost what may. The time of decision has come. Everyone in his right mind knows our beloved Fatherland is on the verge of disaster. The war must be ended *now*. There is only one man who stands in the way of a fair and negotiated peace with the Western Allies. *Adolf Hitler!*' There was a slight metallic pause when a shocked von Dodenburg could hear the faint whir of the recording.

'The Führer, it is clear to all of us who are intimately concerned with the conduct of operations in this war, will not budge from his position. He wants Germany to fight to the bitter end. We cannot allow him to do so. It will mean the total ruination of our Fatherland. Therefore, what is the alternative? I shall tell you.' Even before the speaker revealed his intention von Dodenburg knew what he was going to say, yet when it came, it shocked him beyond measure. *'We must eliminate Adolf Hitler!'*

For what seemed a long time, neither man spoke. Outside, the bombs continued to rain down and the flames flew higher and higher as the high-explosive bombs fanned the fire bombs into a raging fury. Finally Santa Claus asked, 'You know the speaker? He is one of us, of course.'

'Of course.' Von Dodenburg echoed his phrase for some reason he couldn't fathom afterwards. 'It was Field Marshal Erwin Rommel.'

'Exactly. Rommel, our chief, the commander of all our forces in the West. The Führer's one-time favourite soldier.'

'And now the man who wants us to murder him.'

Santa Claus nodded. Outside the flames grew higher and higher . . .

Three

S till dazed by what he had just heard, von Dodenburg came out of the headquarters of the Abwehr in the Tirpitzufer to be confronted by a changed world. For moments, his mind was too full of Rommel's words and the suggestion Santa Claus had made to him – before the former had been urged to report to the shelters at once by his senior adjutant – to take it in.

The whole horizon to the east of the city was ablaze with an evil, flickering, pink light. To his front the tall houses of the middle classes and officialdom trembled and quivered like stage-drops in a high wind. Faces stark with terror, men and women were running frantically for fresh cover, as walls came slithering down in brick and stone avalanches on all sides. Everywhere gas pipes exploded in a gush of searing blue flame. Wardens shrilled their whistles. Police shouted angry orders and waved their rubber clubs. Frightened shouting people, burdened with bundles and rucksacks and whatever else they could find in their frenzied dash for safety, clawed and fought each other to find new shelters.

Von Dodenburg, his lean face already glowing with the heat of the fires, shook his head like someone trying to wake up from a deep sleep. He hesitated to follow the crowd. He didn't like the idea of being forced into a shelter, packed with sweating, scared humanity. But he knew he had to take cover. Sooner or later a policeman or officious warden would come along and order him sharply to go to a shelter.

Then he caught a glimpse of the blue-glowing sign of the

'*U-Bahn*' through a thick brown cloud of drifting smoke. The Berlin Metro. That would do it. The underground possessed more space and it would be orderly, supervised as such places were by soldiers, police and air-raid wardens. He hesitated no longer. Then he was fighting his way down the smelly stairs, already packed with frightened women and snivelling and wailing children, gripping their mothers' hands for all they were worth.

'Can't stay here, *Obersturm*,' a middle-aged policeman shouted politely enough. 'Try Tunnel C . . . Might be lucky there.' And the *Schupo* actually touched his hand to his leather helmet in salute. The gesture slightly amazed von Dodenburg. At least someone was trying to maintain order and discipline in this crazy underground world. Then the lights flickered and went out momentarily before the system kicked back in. But the damage had been done. The crowd started screaming and pushing once more. The *Schupo* disappeared and von Dodenburg told himself that he'd better get to Tunnel C. Otherwise he might well be crushed to death here nearer the surface; that would not be a very worthy end to the one-time commander of SS Assault Regiment Wotan.

He started to push his way down the second flight of stairs. Bombs were dropping directly above now. Time and time again they thudded down. Each time they did so, filling the shelter with the acrid stink of high explosive, the crowd screamed and panicked. Mortar and cement dust trickled down in a grey drizzle. Great clouds of smoke came rushing down the shafts. Now some of the panicked civilians fought to leave the place. 'Keep calm,' the officials yelled. An officer cried, 'It is forbidden to leave the shelter during a raid. Stand fast, I say.' He tried to pull out his pistol to emphasize his order. He didn't get a chance. It was wrenched from his grip. Next moment the crowd swept over him and he went down under their feet, yelling in pain.

Someone slammed into von Dodenburg's wounded shoulder. He yelped and lost his hold on the stairwell. Now he was swept away with the rest, fighting to get to the surface, as the shelter swayed and trembled like a live thing, before it was too late. 'Dammit,' he cried, 'let me go!' Next instant the lights went out and he knew there was no other way than to let himself be carried upwards. Mob violence had taken over.

'Here, take my hand, soldier. I'll help you,' a voice close at hand cried over the screams and cries. A hand seized his. It was warm but dry. The hand's owner, he told himself, was in full control. 'Don't worry . . . I know the way. *Los!*'

'Thank you,' he gasped a little weakly. The pain in his arm was bad. It was as if someone was stabbing his flesh with a red-hot poker, and the arm was wet. He was bleeding again. The blow had probably opened the wound once more. Frail, von Dodenburg let himself be guided.

Up and up they went, clambering and stumbling over abandoned packs and cases and once over a body – though von Dodenburg refused to tell himself that he was actually using a human body to lever himself upwards. Then they were out and gasping in the hot suffocating air, blinking in the blinding light that came from the flames searing the buildings to their front like a gigantic blowtorch.

Von Dodenburg paused and winced with the pain of his arm. 'Thank you,' he choked, turning to his rescuer and exclaiming in surprise. 'But you're – a woman!'

Despite the chaos all around, the young woman, her blonde hair hanging down bedraggled over a dirty face, laughed shortly. She said, 'So I've been told, Mr Officer.' She pressed his hand, which she was still holding protectively. 'Let's get out of this shit mess before the whole shit lot falls on top of us and it's too late.'

'No more shelters!'

'No more shelters, I promise . . . My cellar . . . There we will be safe, I hope. *Now hurry!*'

Supported once more by the young woman, who was dressed in the light grey of the *Wehrmacht*'s female auxiliary, they pushed their way through yet another panicked throng trying to ignore the cries for help, the screams, the curses coming from the civilians trapped in the burning houses on either side of the street.

There were dead bodies everywhere. Lumps of human beings, blown apart, hung from the burning trees which lined the street like human fruit. A head complete with helmet lay in the gutter, next to a dead woman, a dead baby latched on to her limp breast. There was a clatter of hooves. A crazed horse, its tail and mane on fire, dragged a dray behind it, the driver charred black and shrunken to the size of a pygmy, dead on the seat, still holding the reins. Horror upon horror.

Still the unknown blonde wouldn't let herself be deflected. Another gas main exploded. A violent sheet of blue flame gushed upwards, illuminating the soldiers, handkerchieves around their mouths against the stench, trying to sort out a mess of dead children. Weeping hysterically, their mothers watched as they were loaded on to the waiting *Wehrmacht* truck like little logs of charred wood.

'Didn't I tell you, Kumpel,' one of the soldiers was saying, 'the firestorm finishes off all of 'em.' Effortlessly he and his mate tossed another baby on to the back of the truck.

'I heard them screaming,' one of the spectators hushed. She was shaking uncontrollably, as if in the grip of some high fever. 'If there was a God on high He would have shown some mercy on the poor little mites, wouldn't He?'

Next to her, another of the women, hard-eyed, hard-faced, who looked half mad in the flickering light of the burning gas main, said harshly, 'Woman, what are you talking about? . . . Leave God out of this . . . It's not God who makes war, *men do . . . !*' Sickened, confused, in pain, von Dodenburg, one of Germany's most decorated soldiers, the veteran of battles on three continents, a man who had seen more than his share of total war, could do nothing but nod his head in agreement.

An hour later they were making love on the floor of her cellar, the flickering candles magnifying and distorting their sweat-lathered naked bodies. They made love savagely, gripping and biting each other, faces contorted brutally, almost as if they hated each other. Still the bombs rained down. They didn't notice. They continued their frantic pursuit of pleasure, carried away – by what? Not love. Perhaps just a lust for life, the knowledge that they had survived. This time . . .

'They say they are dying all over Berlin now,' she whispered, the beads of sweat in her hair line and eyebrows glistening like opaque pearls. 'I believe it. Even kids, hundreds of them.' She took another drag of her cigarette. 'Kids!' She said the word without emotion. It was as if she was talking about the state of the weather.

He took a drag at his own cigarette, the pain in his arm forgotten now. For the moment he said nothing. He hadn't even asked her name yet – and he didn't think he would do so. What did it matter? He would never see her again. She would become another of his 'conquests', one of the women taken by front swine like himself who were doomed to die sooner or later, needed to eradicate the front swine's sense of loneliness and deprivation. Afterwards the women would be forgotten. It would be almost as if they had never even existed.

'It won't go on for ever,' he attempted.

She turned on him, brushing the dank blonde hair from her high forehead. It was almost as if she were seeing him for the first time. 'How long will it go on for then?' she demanded coldly. 'Till we're all dead perhaps? You, me, the whole of Berlin, the whole of Germany!' She flung open her arms and he could see her breasts once more, the nipples dun-coloured, big and erect. She was at the end of her tether, he could see that. But at the same time, she was sexually excited. Did the two things go together?

Then he, too, was seized by sexual excitement. What else was there left for her, for him? 'Don't talk,' he ordered thickly. 'For God's sake don't talk. The time for talking is over.' He seized her brutally, forgetting the pain in his arm, he was that excited, and pulled her towards him. His nostrils were assailed by the warm animal smell of her body. Her legs parted instinctively. Cruelly he pushed them further apart. She gasped, but did nothing to stop him. Already he was erect. 'Bitch!' he hissed. 'Bitch . . .' He bent and bit her nipple. She cried out. But she didn't stop him. It was almost as if she wanted to feel pain now; as if she felt she deserved it.

His penis nuzzled her. She was wet. Even her inner thighs were wet. He hesitated no longer. With a great grunt, he thrust himself deep inside her. Her spine arched like a taut bow. She moaned and then all else was forgotten in that mad race called Love . . .

Four

K uno von Dodenburg was drunk. He didn't get drunk often – after eight years in the Waffen-SS he had learned how to control his drinking – but this day he had deliberately got drunk. The day had been too disturbing. First there had been 'Santa Claus' and the Rommel message; then that terrible air raid; and then the girl and her totally nihilistic attitude. It had been too much for him.

Now, staggering a little, he made his way back to Lehrter Station through an almost deserted Berlin, though he had the sensation that behind the façade of the locked, blacked-out buildings, ordinary men and women were waiting for the first mournful wail of the air-raid sirens which would herald another night of horror and sudden death. Already the searchlights were sweeping the dark sky with their icy fingers, ready to lock on the first of the 'terror bombers', as the Berliners called the English pilots these days.

Not that von Dodenburg was worried whether he survived this night or not. The drink had calmed him, which he had hoped it would, and stilled the crazy racing of his troubled mind. But it had also left him in a mood of near fatalism. Of course people like his father, the girl, Santa Claus and Field Marshal Rommel were right. Germany was in the process of losing the war and the war could only be stopped by getting rid of the Führer – he preferred not to think of the only way that particular end could be achieved. Yet at that same time many thousands and hundred thousands of brave young men had already given their lives for Hitler's cause. If Germany surrendered now, admitting that she had failed and was nearly defeated, what would the sacrifice of all those youngsters be worth? They had believed in the Führer, the New Order and Germany's mission to reform a corrupt, decadent Europe ruled by equally corrupt old men; and they had given their lives willingly for that belief.

Why, they had marched down this self-same street, six abreast, singing lustily, cheered by the hysterical crowds, Germany's best going to war, heading for the Lehrter and the front from which so many of them would never return. Tears welled up in his red-rimmed eyes as he thought of those young ghosts rotting in some nameless Russian field, forgotten save by their dear ones, these many years now; dead before they had even begun to live. Could he betray their memory and their sacrifice and do what he knew was right: help to bring the war to a speedy end, even if it meant the defeat of the country for which they had died?

He stopped suddenly. He felt an urgent need to urinate. A little drunkenly he fumbled with his flies in the same instant that a blacked-out torch flashed its blue light into his face and an official voice barked, 'What're you up to?'

Von Dodenburg's need was too urgent for him to stop now. He pulled his organ out and started to urinate on the pile of rubble next to a strangely ornate un-German structure. 'I'm taking a piss,' he answered, feeling a sense of relief.

The torch went out and the voice said, 'Sorry, sir, didn't recognize you in the darkness. Thought you might be one of these damned foreign workers, doing a bit of looting. They're everywhere these nights with their dirty, thieving fingers. Mind you, they wouldn't have found much in that place, what's left of it. It's been turned over years ago. Back in '38 in fact. And yer know what the Yids are like. They're cunning swine. They got their stuff out of the country right smartish after the attack.' The fat-bellied policeman touched his fingers to his helmet and departed. 'Watch how you go, sir?' he said over his shoulder, as he flashed his torch back and forth. 'Dangerous place at night, Berlin is these days . . . and there'll probably be one of those terror raids before long . . .' He disappeared into the night, leaving von Dodenburg standing there somewhat stupidly with his penis in his hand, staring at the wall and remembering the time when he had stood at this very spot, baying for blood with the rest of the near hysterical mob . . .

'*Juden Raus . . . Juden Raus . . .*' they had cried in chorus . . . *Jews out!* At the beginning it had been like some good-humoured crowd at a football match, making fun of the visiting team. But that hadn't lasted long when the men of the SA had commenced throwing bricks at the synagogues' windows. That November night so long ago now, the crowd's mood had turned ugly.* They didn't just want the 'Jews out'; after the SA had arrived, they wanted the Jews' blood.

First out had been the rabbi himself. He had obviously prepared himself for the mob inside the threatened synagogue. He had changed into a dark suit and pinned his Iron Cross, won in the First War, on to his chest so the mob baying for Jewish blood could see he had risked spilling his 'tainted' blood for Germany.

The Iron Cross hadn't saved him. A burly Brownshirt had ripped the prized medal from the rabbi's breast, thrust it in his own pocket and with a hefty kick had propelled the cleric into the gutter, where the mob had commenced kicking him. Kuno had never found out whether he had survived that beating. But he could guess that even if the rabbi had, he would have been long murdered somewhere else.

The beating of the rabbi had seemed to be the signal for the wholesale destruction of the synagogue. Yelling at the top of their voices, the Brownshirts had commenced their plundering of the place, urinating on the Torah, destroying what they could not loot, kicking out the Jews they had found

---

*The so-called Crystal Night of 9/10 November 1938, when all of Germany's synagogues had been wrecked.

hiding there, egged on all the time by the baying and cheering of the mob, of which he, Kuno, had been a part.

For what seemed a long time, Kuno stood there in the rubble, staring at the ruined synagogue in the icy light of the searchlights searching the night sky above. His drunkenness seemed to have vanished. Now he felt stone-cold sober – and resigned. He knew now that his fate had been sealed. There was no way out for him. He had been at the start. How could he expect to be saved when his conscience was foul and dirty? Let the plotters do as they wished. If they succeeded, then good luck to them and their plan to save Germany in its darkest hour. He would have to fight on till the bitter end. What was the old saying? *Mitgegangen, mitgefangen, mitgehangen.** That certainly applied to him. Slowly Kuno von Dodenburg turned and walked towards the station and the train that would take him back to France and the battle to come.

As always, twenty-four hours a day, day in, day out, week after week, the great Berlin station was crowded with troops. As the great, black locomotives steamed in and out, bearing the usual legend 'WHEELS ROLL FOR VICTORY' on their boilers, the harsh impersonal voice of the station announcer chanted those destinations which might well mean death to the weary soldiers waiting on the crowded platform.

Sitting in his first-class compartment viewing them, von Dodenburg thought that, heavily laden as they were, they might as well have been Arctic explorers, setting out for a long expedition into the unknown, the poor devils. Now and again the stationmaster in his peaked black cap with the band of his office around his chest would stalk along a train, writing mysterious numbers in chalk on each boxcar, and the waiting men would straighten up, easing on their packs, knowing that they'd be off soon. Their womenfolk, if they were from Berlin, would begin to sniff and reach for

*Literally: 'Went with, caught with, hanged with.'

their handkerchieves. The men would make tut-tutting noises and the lone drunks would jeer if the 'chained dogs' were looking the other way and make obscene suggestions which under the circumstances would be impossible to carry out.

Von Dodenburg sat back in his plush seat. He'd seen it all before – far too often. Now the reaction to the day's events was setting in and he felt tired. Once the train got underway on its long night journey to France, he'd curl up in his greatcoat and, despite the pain in his arm, go to sleep; he needed it.

But that wasn't to be. Just as the announcer high up under the shattered roof began to announce, 'The express for Paris, calling at Saarbrucken, Luxembourg, Metz . . .' the door was slid open hurriedly and another SS officer, carrying a padlocked briefcase, stood there in the dim light to enquire, 'This is First Class?'

Von Dodenburg recognized the voice immediately. It was unmistakable. It was the typical pedantic monotone of a professional schoolteacher. It was that of the Creeper. 'Captain Kriecher,' he snapped. 'What are you doing here in Berlin in three devils' name?'

'Obersturmbannführer,' the Creeper answered, snapping to attention, 'I didn't recognize you in this light.' He raised his head, as if on parade and began to report, '*Sturmbannführer Kriecher meldet sich zur Stelle—*'

'Oh, shut up!' von Dodenburg cut him off sharply. Not only did he not like the Creeper, but he knew that he would have to forgo his sleep; the Creeper, schoolteacher that he had once been, would insist on talking despite the lateness of the hour.

Von Dodenburg was right. As the night 'express' crawled across Germany, stopping in tunnels whenever there was the threat of Allied air attack, detouring into the sidings of the great cities which were being bombed by the British, the Creeper would notice when his travelling companion had woken up and would immediately start talking. Most of his talk was rubbish, pure Party propaganda about the Führer's secret weapons, the imminent break-up of the Western Allied coalition or that Churchill was intent, now that the Red Army had already crossed into Poland, on joining Hitler in the common fight against the Bolsheviks.

Once, the Creeper unwittingly disclosed something of interest. About two that morning after they had been held up by a bombing at Cologne for two hours before the train set off for its original border crossing at Saarbrücken, a weary irate von Dodenburg asked, 'And what exactly was your mission in Berlin, Captain?'

The Creeper smirked, as if he had been waiting for that particular question all along. 'Well, sir, it's very secret and I can't reveal too much about it, even to you, sir, as a senior officer. However, I can say it is something to do with our recent troubles with the French. When the Tommies come we can't have problems to our rear—'

'Oh, come on, Kriecher,' von Dodenburg snapped. 'Don't waffle on . . . like a wet fart waiting to hit the side of the thunderbox. Get on with it.'

The Creeper flushed, but obeyed the harsh command all the same. He said, 'Well, sir, it is clear that the perfidious English have their agents working in the Caen area trying to turn the native against us. And we saw with that air attack that wounded you that the Tommies are prepared to go to great lengths to help these Frog traitors. Reichsführer SS Himmler ordered me to Berlin to discuss the countermeasures which we will take against these French traitors – and I can assure you, sir, that they are going to be very harsh.'

'Oh, I see,' von Dodenburg said and yawned, losing interest. It would be the same old terror tactics: arrest, shooting, burnings, reprisals. They hadn't worked in Russia, Yugoslavia, Poland. They wouldn't work in France. It would only turn more and more French people against the Germans, especially now that it was obvious that the German occupiers were not winning the war. Now the French 'patriots' would be only too eager to curry favour with their new masters to come. He yawned again and closed his eyes, as the train gathered speed, running along the Rhine towards Saarbrücken, and hoped that the Creeper would close his eyes and shut up, too.

But seemingly the Creeper still wanted to chatter. 'There are other things, too, sir, that we discussed in Berlin. It is not only among the Frogs that there are traitors.' The political officer's voice was low and slow now as if he were considering his words carefully. 'There are those among our own ranks, even at the highest levels, who are prepared to betray the Führer. A pack of opportunists, rats ready to abandon the sinking ship . . .'

Von Dodenburg sat up, suddenly very wide awake. He opened his eyes and stared at the other man in the dim, blue light of the stuffy compartment. 'What did you say?'

Von Dodenburg's reaction appeared to act as a warning for the Creeper. 'Nothing of great importance, sir. Just thinking aloud really.' He feigned a yawn. 'To be truthful, I shall be glad to be back in Caen. You see, I've got Lore, my wife, with me there, and I don't like to leave her by herself for too long.' The Creeper frowned and for once, the ex-schoolmaster appeared to be at a loss for words. 'You don't know her, sir, but she is a – er – lively sort of a girl and easily bored. And I don't trust all those young officers and the like. They're very flash with their decorations and all. My Lore can be easily tempted, I'm afraid . . .' His words died away to nothing and there was no sound now save the clatter of the train's wheels and the whistle of it passing through deserted stations. Gradually the Creeper started to snore, lulled into sleep at last.

Not von Dodenburg. On any other occasion he would have laughed at the Creeper and his problems with a frisky, bored wife, probably half his age. But not now. The Creeper's words about highly placed traitors had unsettled him. He had thought he had left Berlin and all its complicated problems behind him. He hadn't. He was bringing the problems of what was to be done – whether the Führer would have to be assassinated, whether an attempt should be made to reach a separate peace with the Tommies while there was still time – with him. Kuno von Dodenburg groaned inwardly. God in heaven, why couldn't he have the brutal simplicity of the fighting front where these considerations were totally unimportant and one concentrated on the bloody business of combat. At that moment, he felt like praying that the Tommies would invade now and be done with it . . .

Five

Lore Kriecher – 'my little cabbage', as the Creeper called her fondly – was neither little nor a cabbage. She was big, blonde, blowsy and usually bored in a country where she couldn't speak a word of the language, save '*ne comprends pas*' and there were no handy *Gasthauses* or cafés where a thirsty woman – and she was often thirsty – might get a quick beer or a slab of ersatz cream cake.

Not that Lore Kriecher was bored this particular night. As her husband's train crawled ever closer to Caen, bringing back the total bore, she was intent on having a good time, even if it meant missing her 'beauty sleep' as she called it. Her husband would want 'it', too, when he came home in the morning, but she'd soon settle him; his needs were small just like his anatomy below the belt. Indeed it took all her willpower not to yawn when he was doing 'it' with her, and more than once she had fallen asleep during the act while he puffed and panted, his face brick red and his pince-nez steamed up, looking as if he might have a heart attack at any moment; and sometimes Lore wished he would. Then she'd get a widow's pension and she could return to her home in Westphalia, where there were still enough hams and plump sausages to be obtained on the black market if you had the wherewithal.

But now Lore concentrated on enjoying herself and it wasn't a plump Westphalian sausage that would be her particular pleasure this night; it was the equally plump one of Senior Sergeant Schulze. Naked save for his 'dice-beakers',

87

a glass of good Munich 'suds' in one hand and a Vulkan contraceptive – a 'Volcano', meant for extra strong eruptions – he lectured the equally naked and drunken Lore on the 'drill'. 'First yer take off my dice-beakers, my little cheetah, then you position yersen on that sofa with yer back to the wall and then I'll ram it to you and you better hold on tight, 'cos I'm in one of my moods tonight, beloved.' He rolled his red-rimmed eyes enticingly.

She breathed out hard, but it wasn't the rolling of Sergeant Schulze's bloodshot eyes that excited her, it was that thing sticking up like a policeman's truncheon between his legs. 'Will you do piggeries to me?' she hushed excitedly. Hastily she took a swallow of her beer from the litre mug of the Munich 'suds' that she was holding.

'Anything your heart desires, light of my life,' Schulze said airily. 'Now the dice-beakers, beloved.'

She put down her mug hastily, as if she couldn't get started on 'the drill' soon enough. She dropped from the sofa, turned and straddled herself over his left jackboot, her plump backside towards him, her rosy cheeks set in what a joyful drunken Schulze thought was a very inviting pose. Playfully, he slapped her bottom and she giggled, simpering, 'You naughty boy, you simply can't wait for it, can you?'

'You can say that again, little sweet one,' Schulze said. At the back of his head a cynical little voice rasped, 'Go on, slip her a big link of sausages and think that yer getting something that arse-with-ears, the Creeper, will never get.' It was a thought that made Schulze more excited than ever. Lore would be good plain fare, unlike the kind of *'ooh-la-la'* naughty-naughty stuff that the French girls in Fifi's knocking shop dished out. But the thought of revenge on the hated Creeper made it just as exciting.

Schulze placed his left foot against her buttocks and pressed hard. With a grunt she pulled off the big leather boot and dropped it to the carpet, saying, 'The next one. And don't stick your foot so deep up my crotch. It hurts.'

'Don't tell me you don't like it to hurt, beloved.'

She giggled again, her breasts wobbling like big puddings as she did so. 'The things you say. You make a poor innocent maiden from Westphalia blush red with your coarse soldier's talk, you do.'

He slapped her bottom playfully once more and chortled. 'When a man's busy fighting for his country, darling, he forgets his manners, and how to treat the ladies. Please forgive my rough soldier's ways.' He pushed hard again and she slammed on to the floor, boot still in her hands, rump in the air, revealing that she wasn't a true blonde.

Schulze's eyes nearly popped out of his head at the sight. 'All that meat and no potatoes,' he sighed, using the old soldier's expression. 'By the Great Rabbi of Lodz and all his foreskins, a soldier could die happy scaling that mountain of flesh.'

Lore pulled herself together. She turned and faced him and after taking a bite of her sausage and washing down the spicy meat with a swallow of beer from the litre mug, she simpered, 'I hope you're not going to take advantage of a simple country girl, Sergeant Schulze, a poor innocent who has never done anything quite like this before.' She opened her legs slightly and later Sergeant Schulze would swear to Corporal Matz that something had seemed to be lurking there, ready to leap out at any moment and drag him in.

'Of course not,' Schulze declared gallantly. 'I'd marry you this very day if it were not for the fact that you are married to a prick – er,' he corrected himself hastily, '– to another.'

'An officer too,' she chided.

'And an officer, too,' he echoed. 'But let us not waste no more words, beloved. Seeing you thus, I tremble with uncontrollable passion.'

'Do you?' she quavered.

'I do,' he swore.

'Then come, my dearest.' She extended her arms and now he could see the matted tangle of thick black hair under her armpits which confirmed that she wasn't really a true blonde. 'Take me . . . I am yours. For ever.'

But Lore Kriecher was not fated to be Sergeant Schulze's for ever or even for this particular night. Abruptly the two star-crossed lovers were startled out of their wits by a thunderous knock at the door. Lore put her hands across her magnificent breasts, crying, 'It's him! He's come to shoot us.'

Sergeant Schulze wasn't impressed. 'Shoot us!' he grunted. 'That frigger couldn't hit a barn door with a bayonet.' Next moment he was less impressed when the familiar voice of Corporal Matz, his old running mate, hissed urgently, 'Hands off yer cock and on with yer socks, Schulzi. Get out here. There's something going on and it's after frigging curfew.'

'Can't a poor old hairy-assed stubble-hopper enjoy his simple pleasures in peace,' he moaned, 'without being disturbed. *Verpiss' dich, Mensch!'*

But Corporal Matz was not going to 'piss off'. There was something going on and he'd known Schulze too long to let him be murdered in this little love-nest just like that. 'Pull on yer frigging knickers,' he snarled. 'The Frogs are acting up. There's no time to lose.'

Lore wailed, 'Don't leave me, dear Sergeant Schulze.' She clutched desperately at him, as he started to pull on his dice-beakers. 'God only knows what those Frogs will do to a poor defenceless woman like me. They say they're totally perverted.' In her acute distress, she took an unusually large bite of her sausage and started to choke with coughing.

Schulze ignored her. He could hear the shooting now, recognizing the high-pitched hysterical burr of an MG42, the standard German machine gun, interspersed with the slower *tick-tick* of a British Bren gun, sounding a little like an irate woodpecker. He flung open the door. Matz was standing there. His eyes bulged from his head when he saw the naked woman cowering on the couch, revealing all her opulent fleshy charms. 'Great crap on the Christmas tree!'

he exclaimed. 'Will yer cast yer glassy orbits on them tits! Why, a bloke could get his head between those milk factories and never know no pain for days on end.'

'Knock it off,' Schulze growled. 'Where's the frigging fire?'

But he didn't need Matz's answer. For he could see himself from whence the trouble was coming. To the west, where the Norman coast lay, solid pillars of grey smoke were rising in the still night sky, illuminated by the silver light of the spectral moon; and from the same direction came the angry snap and crackle of a small-arms fight. 'The invasion?' he snapped.

'Doubt it,' Matz answered, tearing his eyes away from Lore's naked body with difficulty. 'The Frogs are acting up, I think. We're the duty NCOs. We'd better take our hind legs in our hands toot sweet and find out what's going on before the orderly officer makes an appearance.'

Schulze nodded his agreement. Turning to the terrified woman, he blew her a juicy kiss and cried, 'Beloved, farewell. Wait for me, I shall return.' He blew her another kiss, as Matz winked lasciviously and whispered, 'If he don't come back, little lady, Corporal Matz, your humble servant, would be only too glad to oblige.' The little Bavarian made an obscene gesture with his finger to ensure that she would know exactly how he would like to oblige her.

But Frau Kriecher was too terrified to be interested in sex at this particular moment. She padded hurriedly to the door, locked and bolted it, and then, as an afterthought, she fetched her husband's duck gun, which he used to hunt the bird in the Dives marshes, and retreated to the couch, the gun across her naked legs ready for use. It would be thus, naked apart from a pair of black silk knickers, trimmed with red lace that he had never seen her wear before, that a suddenly very suspicious Creeper found her on his arrival next morning.

It was about that time when the Creeper was crying at

his wife, 'For God's sake, Lore, must you sit around like that . . . like some five-mark Berlin whore?!' that a weary von Dodenburg reported to the hospital to have his newly opened wound attended to. As tired as he was, the tall, lean SS colonel was happy to see that Nurse Bogex was on duty as the senior nurse. As soon as she saw him, she dropped what she was doing and came rushing up, flushed and angry in the prettiest way, tut-tutting and saying, '*Now* what have you done, General? Letting your wound open like that. Stand still. I'll pour some iodine on it immediately. It'll sting and no doubt you deserve it, if it does.'

Von Dodenburg laughed. 'You do make a man welcome, Sister Bogex. What have I done to expect so much love from you, nuisance that I am?'

If von Dodenburg had expected the French nurse to laugh at his remark, he was badly mistaken. Even as he winced with the pain of the iodine she was dribbling into his wound, he could see the tears well up in her pretty dark eyes, as she mumbled that he shouldn't talk to her like that; she was doing her best.

His face became serious, his pain suddenly forgotten. 'Of course you do, Sister. I have never had a better nurse during this war – and especially one so pretty.'

Now she blushed and with his free hand, he pushed up her chin gently so that she was looking him directly in the eye. She tried to twist her head, but he wouldn't let her. Instead he kept her there, as she continued to pour the iodine, the yellow disinfectant now spilling on to the floor, though she didn't notice it, it seemed. 'You couldn't have done more for me, Yvette,' he said tenderly, using her first name for the very first time, 'if you had been one of our German nurses. You have treated me well, you have treated me well . . .' He ended a little lamely, feeling that somehow he was getting out of his depth.

'You are a wounded man. For me it is the same whether you are German or French. You are sick. You must be helped!' Now her voice lacked that determined, professional tone that he had associated with her ever since he had first been treated by Nurse Bogex. Suddenly he had a feeling that Nurse Bogex felt more for him than just being his nurse. Yet, for some reason he couldn't quite fathom, she was ashamed for having such feelings.

But von Dodenburg, a little puzzled as he was, had no further time to discuss the matter with the pretty French nurse, busy now, placing another bandage on his reopened wound. For in that instant, the smart stamp of heavy boots hurrying down the hospital corridor alerted him once again to the fact that something strange was going on in the area held by Witt's 'Baby Division' – he had already seen the corpses of killed young SS men outside the hospital when he had arrived there thirty minutes before, and an unshaven Corporal Matz, who had been in charge of them, had whispered out of the side of his mouth as his CO had passed inside, 'Trouble, sir . . . bad trouble.'

Now the 'bad trouble' caught up with him in the form of an elegant general's aide, who clicked his highly polished boots together, saluted and slightly bowed from his tight waist to announce, 'The General requests you attend him immediately outside, sir. He has something of importance to show you.'

Von Dodenburg took a look at Nurse Bogex, but she had bent her head again and he couldn't see her eyes. Gently he released himself from her grip, saying, 'Thank you, nurse. Perhaps I shall see you again,' and without waiting for her reply, he elbowed the aide to help him into his tunic and escort him outside into the fine May sunshine.

Six

Standartenführer Witt was in a rage. As he spoke, his fat jowl wobbled visibly and he fingered his pistol holster constantly, as if he would dearly love to draw his pistol and shoot somebody – anybody. In a way, von Dodenburg, watching the Hitler Youth's staff officers visiting the scene of the slaughter, could understand. Witt's 'Babies' had walked straight into a trap and had been virtually massacred without having any real chance to defend themselves.

Now the Division's engineers and medics were recovering more of the innocents' dead bodies from the Dives swamp, pulling them out of the area, which the Division had itself flooded as a pre-invasion measure, with a dreadful sucking sound. Then the medics went to work, cleaning their ashen young faces of mud as the first step to their identification.

Yet in this instant as he stood on the hillock with Schulze and Matz, forgetting the cost in human life, he considered the massacre of the Hitler Youth patrol a justification of his own attitude to the 'Baby Division'. The enthusiastic teenage volunteers were no match for trained soldiers or the French partisans who had obviously carried out the atrocity, luring the patrol into the swamp, where whoever had been in charge had lost control of his men and their combined firepower and it had become a confused mess, with every man trying to save himself.

'Poor shits,' Schulze said after a while, as yet another body was dumped in the grass and a medic started to clean the face with a hosepipe attached to the water truck. 'They should have

94

looked behind themselves.' The words seemed unfeeling –
Sergeant Schulze was not given to sentimentality; he had seen
too much of combat – but they did express von Dodenburg's
feelings. 'Yes, Schulze, poor shits . . . Come on, let's get a
little closer.'

They moved nearer to where Witt stood lecturing his group
of angry staff officers and where von Dodenburg could now
see the reason for the patrol's march right into their death
trap. Some fifty metres to their front at the edge of the
flooded Dives area, a line of so-called 'Rommel asparagus'
– stout beams some three metres high with mines placed on
their tops – had been set alight. Now the devices, intended
to rip the wings of any enemy gliders attempting to land here
between the Rivers Dives and Orne and help form a barrier to
stop the German 15th Army coming to assist their comrades
of the German 7th Army in case of an English invasion, stood
there like giant blackened matchsticks.

For a moment von Dodenburg forgot the dead being hauled
out of the swamp and stared at the beams thoughtfully.
'Why?' he asked half-aloud.

'Why what, sir?' Schulze asked.

Ten metres away one of the mud-splattered engineers was
crying, 'There's one seems to be alive here, gentlemen . . .
Get some rope – *quick*.'

'Why set those poles alight in the first place? I mean
the French could have found some other way of attracting
the patrol's attention?' Then he dropped the subject as the
engineer who had shouted waded into the mud and bent
down to clean the youth's face, pulling the mud out of the
poor soldier's mouth to prevent him being choked, as they
dragged him out by means of the rope. Hastily von Dodenburg
ran forward to help, followed by Schulze and Matz.

But even as he reached the spot, he could see there was no
hope for the poor boy. Someone had attempted to administer
the *coup de grâce* to the back of his skull. The slug hadn't
killed him outright, but now the exposure, the hours spent

in the swamp and the lack of immediate medical attention meant, as Schulze expressed it in his usual brutalized fashion, 'He ain't got a chance. He'll snuff it within the hour.' And as he watched the boy being dragged to the firmer area and the staff followed Standartenführer Witt to see what was going on, all that von Dodenburg could do was to nod his head in agreement.

Witt himself cradled the dying boy's head in his arm and tried to force some brandy from his own silver flask between his lips. But the boy turned his head to one side, croaking, 'Don't drink, sir . . . Try to keep fit . . . all the time.'

Listening, Schulze shook his head in disbelief. What could one make of these boys who only drank milk; what kind of cardboard soldiers were they?

'*Es lebe unser Führer Adolf Hitler!*'* the boy cried suddenly. His spine arched like a taut bowstring. Next moment he fell back into Standartenführer Witt's arms – dead. Gently the general lowered the body to the ground and ran his now muddy hand across the dead boy's forehead, smoothing back his long blond hair.

For a moment there was a heavy silence, broken only by the sound of the wind from the Channel ruffling the surface of the river and the harsh breathing of the engineers as they hauled another victim out of the mud. Here and there a seagull rose watching like a child seeking a lost mother. Watching, von Dodenburg knew that Witt wasn't a sensitive man. Commanders of SS divisions, especially one consisting of unblooded teenagers, couldn't afford to be. They would be unable to send their 'men' into combat and possibly to their death. Yet he could see that the fat *Standartenführer* was moved, and with emotion came an ever-growing anger.

Slowly Witt rose to his feet. His staff stared at him. Controlling himself with difficulty, his fists clenched, Witt said: 'We must make an example.'

*'Long live our Leader, Adolf Hitler.'

There was a murmur of agreement. The Creeper, whose face was now bruised for some reason that von Dodenburg couldn't fathom, said, 'I have advocated that all along, *Standartenführer.*'

No one took any notice of the statement. Witt said, almost as if he were talking to himself, thinking on his feet, 'We shall take hostages. In the city. Ten for every one of my poor boys slaughtered so treacherously . . . We shall give the killing swine forty-eight hours to come forward. If they don't, you know what to do.'

With a nod he indicated that his officers should return to their vehicles. Von Dodenburg hesitated. For a moment he was inclined to protest against the hostage business; it wouldn't work, he knew that now. But he, too, had been moved by the dying boy and his loyalty in the moment of his death – '*es lebe der Führer*'. The kid hadn't deserved to die like that. In the end he decided he'd talk to Witt some other time and perhaps not even then. He turned to the two NCOs. 'All right you rogues, let's have a look at those beams . . .'

For once they didn't ask why. The mood was too sombre. While the engineers hauled out another body, grunting as they tugged at the rope like fishermen tired out with a big catch, the three of them began to squelch through the mud towards the burned-out beams . . .

'They're a lot of wet-tails, soft wet-tails,' Schulze cried contemptuously, as he settled his old hares down. 'Too much frigging milk and too much of the one-handed widow.' He made a gesture as if he were masturbating with his hamlike fist.

No one of the fifty or more corporals and sergeants assembled in the Hitler Youth gym laughed. Their mood, too, was too sombre. All of them had heard of the massacre and already the 'chained dogs' were busy in the city, they knew, rounding up the hostages. Sentries were posted everywhere at key military installations and the Caen Chief of Police, as supposed enthusiastic collaborator, had been arrested. Danger and tension lay in the very air.

Schulze went on, warming to his theme. 'But we can't let the poor soft kids be slaughtered like this. After all we are supposed to be the Führer's Fire Brigade, SS Assault Regiment Wotan, or what's frigging left of it. It's our duty to go and get our stupid big turnips shot off for the Führer.'

This time the big NCO did get a hollow, cynical laugh from some of his audience. The old hares had long lost their enthusiasm for the Führer and his New Order, just like Schulze had. 'Follow the Führer – he's got a hole in his arse,' One Ball cried, getting carried away a little by Schulze's inflammatory words, and, next to him, Flipper slapped his wooden arm down hard and yelled in support, 'That's the stuff to give the troops, Schulzi. A bottle of firewater and some suds thrown in and I'd tackle the buck-teethed Tommies' whole tea-drinking army with my one arm. You can believe that, old house.'

It was at that juncture that von Dodenburg strode into the gym purposefully and full of determination, his gloomy mood of the last few days cast aside. 'I didn't hear that remark,' he called, as Schulze prepared to call the men to attention. He shook his head and said, 'After what happened this morning, there's no time for that kind of bullshit. Stay seated.'

He wasted no time. Indicating that Schulze should step to one side and allow him to address the old hares personally, he launched straight in to the reason why he had summoned them to assemble here this evening. 'Comrades, you all know what happened to those poor devils of the "Baby Division" last night. Personally I don't think the Resistance deliberately lured that patrol into a trap. There was something else involved. I'll tell you more in a few minutes. All the same, a massacre *did* take place, one that *I – you –* will not allow to happen again.'

There was a mumble of agreement from the old hares. Someone growled, 'Them milk-drinkers couldn't even get laid in a knocking shop, they're so frigging innocent. They should still be at their mother's titty.'

Von Dodenburg allowed himself a wintry smile. 'No doubt you're right, Krause. So we have a duty to ensure that those young fellows return to – er – their mother's titty in one piece. How are we going to do it? There are not more of us than – say – two hundred old hares left.' He answered his own question. 'This way. When the English drop their paras, which undoubtedly they will, we're going to stop them. Then there can be no link-up between these English parachutists and their seaborne infantry coming in from the coast.'

'But, sir,' Matz objected, 'how can we know where these Tommies are going to drop? Normandy's a big place.'

'I know, Corporal, but I think I can guess where they will drop, in general. Most of our officers can make the same guess. On the line of the Rivers Dives–Orne. But again that river line is long. So where will their drop zones be?' He paused and let his question sink in. 'I'll tell you. Where those poor unfortunates were dragged out of the mud this morning. It's swampy and a most unlikely spot for a DZ. So why did the French Resistance set those beams afire at that particular place? A, to check if they present an effective deterrent to a gliderborne attack. B, because they wanted to draw our attention to the swampy nature of the terrain and make it clear to us it was such an unlikely spot.'

Schulze whistled softly and said, 'Sounds reasonable to me, sir. But how are you going to convince Standartenführer Witt of that, sir?'

Von Dodenburg turned on him. 'Schulze, you big rogue,' he declared, face set in a grim smile. 'I'm not, frankly. This is what I'm going to do instead . . .'

Five or ten minutes later, as the May sun started to go down in the west, colouring the sky over the Channel, from which the invasion would come one day soon, a deep blood red, they left, bearing von Dodenburg's secret with them. But there was none of the usual chatter of men released from some military conference, heading for a beer of the simple, brutal pleasures of front swine. Instead they were silent, each man wrapped in a cocoon of his own thoughts and apprehensions.

Von Dodenburg was alone and thoughtful, his pace slow, as he realized that he was committed now. Those vague hints of treachery and assassination of the last few days were thrust to the back of his mind. But he knew that his own plan to take action without orders from above and against the Führer's own express wish might well be construed as treason, too, if it didn't work. But that didn't matter. In the overall picture, his personal fate was of no importance. His task now was to save what was left of Wotan and as many of those milk-drinking kids of the 'Baby Division' as possible. That was about it.

Watching him cross the parade ground from her own tiny garret room of the German-occupied hospital, Nurse Bogex sighed a little helplessly. What would happen to him soon? she asked herself. She shook her dark head, tears suddenly in her eyes. Then she continued with her packing. The Germans were moving her and all the other nurses who were French to the Convent of St-Saveur, which had a large hospital, too. The German general had ordered there would be no more unnecessary contact between his troops and the French civilians.

She closed her shabby case on her few belongings and tested the weight. It wasn't too heavy. Besides she knew when 'it' happened and she was forced to flee, she didn't want to be carrying any unnecessary weight. God only knew how long that flight would take. But she'd leave a note for him, at least. He mustn't think she'd abandoned him.

Up in his hiding place, the Creeper lowered his powerful binoculars, as she started to scribble something on a pad and von Dodenburg disappeared round the corner, heading in the direction of the officers' mess. Now he knew, he told himself. There was something going on between the two of them, the French nurse and that arrogant bastard, von Dodenburg. His type always had their way with pretty women. Slowly he stuffed his glasses away in their case and replaced his pince-nez at the top of his beaky nose.

He rose, but didn't move off. He wanted to savour his triumph before he went home to Lore, who undoubtedly by this time would be drinking beer by the litre and stuffing herself full of those spicy Westphalian sausages that her goddam farmer father sent her from his farm near Warendorf. *She'd* naturally pour cold waters on any of his achievements. So it was no use telling her anything of what he felt he had discovered.

He sniffed like he had done before the war, entering a classroom that seemed to stink of unwashed, cheeky boys. One day, however, she'd be proud of him, he told himself. There might even be a medal in it for him when he revealed to the authorities what he believed was going on: the unspeakable treachery of high-ranking officers, even those of the SS, and these unspeakable French who were working with them to bring about the downfall of Germany's glorious 1,000-year-old Reich.

He smiled suddenly, though as always, his mean little eyes didn't light up. Perhaps Lore might spoil him in bed tonight after all. He'd been home two days now from Berlin and it was about time. Wasn't he a man, master in his own home? He wouldn't *ask*; he would *demand* his conjugal rights. Yessir, that he would!

His body surging with new purpose, the Creeper left his hiding place, watched by Sergeant Schulze, who tugged at the front of his trousers purposefully, telling himself the little arsehole was up to something. What it was didn't really matter. All that mattered was that the Creeper wasn't going to cut a slice of Lore's plump Westphalian sausage this night. He'd seen to that. She'd had more than enough of his 'links' this afternoon to ensure that she'd need nothing more in that area this night. He grinned maliciously and then, well satisfied with the way things were going, the big NCO headed for the sergeants' wet canteen and the usual row of six beers and six schnapps lined up on the pristine bar, waiting for him there.

And thirty kilometres away on the other side of that Channel which separated two worlds, as if they were earth and moon, so remote from each other, the bobbing invasion armada started to fill the harbours and ports everywhere along England's south coast. For four long years the men who would sail in that armada had waited for this day of revenge and retribution. Soon they would sail, rank upon rank of them, ten miles wide, each lane twenty miles across, five thousand ships bearing 180,000 young men, heading for the shores of Adolf Hitler's vaunted *Festung Europa*, while in that Fortress other young men – and older ones – played their doomed games . . .

BOOK THREE

Sie Kommen!

He was a different man. Something had come to him, which had not yet come to us. It was the trial of battle and no one who passes through it is ever quite the same again.

H. Allen

One

As May 1944 gave way to June, the tension started to mount in the German camp. Intelligence was convinced that it would be this summer when the Western Allies would launch their invasion of Europe. Together with the Command's weathermen, they closely studied the forecasts for the month of June and tried to assess when there would be high tides. For they were convinced that the enemy would launch his assault at high tide. The 'Tommies' wouldn't repeat the mistake they had made at Dieppe two years before when the enemy naval force had landed the troops too far out; most of them had been slaughtered even before they got close enough to the German defences to attack.

At the same time as Rommel's Intelligence tried to out-guess the Allies and fix dates when the enemy would attack, the Field Marshal, once known as 'the Desert Fox' when he had fought and lost to the British General Montgomery in Africa, intensified his preparations on the beaches for that attack. Everywhere in Normandy and elsewhere along the French coast as far as the Spanish border, huge working parties of German engineers, French workers and forced labourers worked 24-hour shifts to improve the defences of what Hitler was now calling his 'Atlantic Wall'. Meanwhile Rommel tried to persuade Hitler to release to him the panzer divisions now stationed in France so that he, Rommel, could decide when they should be thrown into the coming battle.

But Hitler at his lair in the Bavarian Alps, over 600 kilometres from the French coast, remained adamant. He would retain control of the German armour and *he* would decide when and where it should be employed. For as Hitler stonewalled an irate Rommel over and over again with the same old phrase, 'But, my dear Rommel, what if the enemy launches a feint – the English are a cunning race as you know – and we throw in all our armour, and what does he do then? Why, he launches his main attack elsewhere. Then, Rommel, we will have lost the Battle of France. No, my dear Rommel, we cannot be too hasty and premature.'

But Hitler's 'dear Rommel' had other plans for that armour than employing it against the man who had beaten him in Africa, Montgomery. Rommel wanted every important unit stationed in France under his personal command, even the SS divisions if he could manage it. As he told his fellow conspirators, 'When the time comes to remove the Führer –' even Rommel dared not speak the word 'assassinate', which was the plotters' real intention – 'I want total control of our forces in the West. It is the only way that we can negotiate with the Western Allies and convince them they can land in France without having to fire a single shot. We'll worry about the Eastern Front when we have secured a peace with Churchill.'

While Rommel and the rest of the *Wehrmacht* generals prepared for the invasion, yet at the same time planned Hitler's murder and a separate peace with the enemy in the west, Obersturmbannführer Kuno von Dodenburg readied the 'babies' of the Hitler Youth Division for their baptism of fire. The teenage volunteers thought of themselves, in the words of their own motto, 'as fleet of foot as a greyhound, as hard as leather, as tough as steel' – after all, they had been training for this ever since they had been kids in short pants – but they had never encountered trainers such as Sergeant Schulze, Corporal Matz and the rest of von Dodenburg's old hares. Now under the command of the lean hard-faced SS colonel, the old hares ran the 'babies' ragged from dawn to dusk, and this June there was no more milk being served to the 'babies'.

As Sergeant Schulze was wont to address them at the beginning of every day's training, standing there in the dawn light, legs spread, hands on hips, staring at their bronzed, earnest young faces with a look of unbelievable contempt, 'You're just a bunch of wet-tails, soft shits the lot of yer, full of piss and vinegar. Up to now you've had it cushy, pushed an easy ball, playing cardboard soldiers.' He spat into the cropped, burned grass. 'Soldiers like you – by the Great Whore of Buxtehude, where the dogs piss sideways – I've shat before breakfast.' He slapped his horny palm against the side of the brand-new Panther tank and made his listeners jump. 'But it's got to stop. By all that is holy to me and Corporal Matz here, we've got to stop it. Great crap on the Christmas tree, we'll stop it, won't we, Corporal, if it's the last thing we ever do!' He paused for breath, his massive chest heaving in and out with the effort of so much talk at the top of his voice.

'You're right,' Corporal Matz chimed in. 'The Führer expects no less from us, Sergeant Schulze.'

Schulze crossed himself swiftly, which puzzled the 'babies', all of whom had long given up on religion. 'Amen to that, Corporal Matz.'

'Yer might have broken yer mothers' hearts,' Matz shouted in his thick Bavarian accent, 'but you won't break ours. 'Cos our hearts are made of frozen ice . . .'

Watching the performance, von Dodenburg told himself that a casual observer might think the two NCOs meant it. In reality, however, it was just a carefully calculated performance. Their rage was artificially meant to frighten the 'babies' into instant obedience; to sting them into some sort of reaction, any reaction, as long as it was positive and meant swift, unthinking action.

Now Schulze took over again. 'Now listen here, you piss-pansies. Behind me you'll see a 37mm anti-tank gun, old and not very powerful, but it can give yer a nasty pain in the arse, if it hits yer there. Next to me –' again he slapped the steel hide of the Panther – 'the Division's most powerful tank with a frontal glacis plate that no known anti-tank gun can penetrate. That peashooter behind me can fire at a range of one hundred metres and its shells will bounce off the Panther like ping-pong balls.' He let the information sink in, while his young listeners wondered where all this was leading.

They soon found out.

'Now every one of you wet-tails will take a little drive in the turret of the Panther to where that gun is waiting for you. It will fire at you *direct* and undoubtedly you'll cream yer skivvies.' Schulze smirked and repeated the phrase; he liked the sound of it. 'But you'll do it and see what it's like to be under real fire, fire that will lop off yer silly frigging turnips if you make a mistake in a real tank battle. Now to your stations!'

For a moment the 'babies' seemed rooted to the spot, as if they were realizing what the order entailed: they were going to risk their lives. But iron discipline of the SS prevailed and they broke ranks and doubled away to their stations and the other waiting 46-ton tanks.

For a moment von Dodenburg had seen enough. But naturally he wanted to harden these young men and teach them what real combat was like. At the same time, they were training in the area where he had planned they would fight if the enemy airborne landing took place here as he thought it would. By the time he had finished with them, the 'babies' would know every hill, every tree, bush, indeed anything upon which to mark a target immediately and its range. For von Dodenburg knew the man who fired first usually won.

Leaving the trainees to get on with their first action under live fire, he was about to set off towards the marshes once again when a Volkswagen jeep nosed its way around the corner of the country road to deposit the Creeper immediately in his path. Von Dodenburg frowned. The ex-schoolteacher seemed to be here, there and everywhere these days, ever since he had returned from Berlin. In a way von Dodenburg guessed what he was up to, but he didn't like the way the Leadership Officer was always turning up unexpectedly at his own command.

The Creeper clicked to his attention and reported. Von Dodenburg touched his hand casually to his battered old SS cap and said, 'What brings you here, Captain – *again*?'

But as always, irony was wasted on the Creeper. The latter said, 'I am just carrying out my duties as Leadership Officer, sir.'

Von Dodenburg looked him up and down, as he might some slovenly new recruit. 'I thought I was the leader here, Captain.'

Now the Creeper actually blushed. 'I didn't mean it in that sense, sir. I meant it to—'

He didn't finish his sentence. The 37mm shell slammed into the side of the Panther just as the driver had panicked and turned sideways too early. Instead of hitting the steep glacis plate and bouncing off like a glowing golfball, the armour-piercing anti-tank shell ploughed through the thinner metal, making it glow an ugly red for an instant before burrowing its way into the tank. That angry sound of steel striking steel was followed a moment later by a muted boom. Abruptly the tank came to a stop, rearing up on its bogies like a wild horse being put to saddle for the first time. White smoke started to seep from the closed turret hatch.

'Oh my God!' the Creeper wailed. 'What have you done to my young men, *Obersturm*? Have you killed them with your unconventional methods—?'

'Oh, shut your damnfool mouth!' Von Dodenburg pushed the other man to one side and sprinted over to the stalled Panther, while Schulze was already clambering up the side, burning his hands as he did so, tugging at the turret hatch with all his strength.

'I shall be forced to report this incident to Standartenführer Witt when he gets back from Paris!' the Creeper shouted after the running officer.

'Stick it up your mean little arse,' von Dodenburg called over his shoulder and then he, too, was tugging at the jammed hatch, nostrils assailed by the smell of burnt flesh . . .

Time was running out for von Dodenburg and his old hares. That was clear to everyone under his command. Every day he stepped up the pressure: platoon attacks, company attacks, battalion-sized attacks, night attacks, anti-partisan attacks, attacks supporting infantry . . . hour after hour from dawn to dusk, when the June sun finally sank behind the horizon and the 'babies' could stagger off blindly to their bunks to collapse and fall into an exhausted sleep immediately.

Even when the 'babies' had their short midday break and spooned their thick Giddy-up Soup ravenously, there was no respite for them. The old hares would regale them with the lore of the battlefield. 'When an enemy tank comes at yer, don't piss yer knickers. Blind him with your headlights straight off or give him a couple of star shells to put him off his aim . . . Wait till the tank breasts a rise and shows yer his soft bottom, then slip him a shell there like you might to yer girlfriend – that is, those of you who like girls . . . Flank 'em . . . allus flank . . . this Panther of ours can tackle a whole squadron of them Shermans of theirs from the flank . . . That's why we call 'em the Ronson – one flick and they're alight . . . Never go into combat with yer hatch open. Some buck-teethed Tommy is more than likely to toss a grenade in and there goes yer turnip . . .' Lesson after lesson, taught with the cynical brutality of men who had survived this long because of that same cynical brutality: men who did not accept the fatalism of the average stubble-hopper, but who knew all the dirty tricks of their calling and were prepared to use them to save their own hides.

But von Dodenburg's harsh unremitting training took its toll on the old hares, too. Corporal Matz discovered, for example, that M'selle Fifi's famed 'knee-tremblers' carried out swiftly and efficiently in any convenient doorway were not only costing him too much money, but were wearing him out, too. Even Sergeant Schulze, that star performer at dancing the 'Mattress Polka' as part of the 'two-backed beast', found that Lore was just a little too much when she demanded it a third time on the occasions when she could escape the Creeper's constant suspicions. 'Why, Matzi, she's even bringing me ham and sausage now,' he confided a little miserably to his old running mate, 'to build me up, as she says. Build me frigging up! How can she build me up when the CO's frigging well building me down all day long?'

It was a question that Matzi, 'the Bavarian barn-shitter', could not answer.

Nor could the Creeper. For he, too, spent most of his days this first week of June trying to keep an eye on his wife Lore and, at the same time, collecting ever more evidence that he would use against the arrogant Obersturmbannführer von Dodenburg one day – and one day soon for Headquarters had informed him that no less a person than Obergruppenführer Sepp Dietrich, the officer who had formed the first major *Waffen SS* formation and now the SS Panzer Corps commander, was coming from Paris with Witt to inspect the 'Baby Division'.

As the Creeper saw it, who better to report to than Dietrich, the stocky tough Bavarian Party bully boy, who was a personal friend of the Führer. He would surely be very receptive to any information about the wrong kind of training in the wrong place currently being carried out by that swine von Dodenburg. Besides, what would Dietrich say to a senior SS officer who seemingly had a dubious friendship with a Frenchwoman who might well be working for their damned treacherous back-stabbing Resistance? The Creeper could guess. Dietrich wouldn't like it one bit – and when Dietrich didn't like something, the sparks flew.

Two

They shot the first batch of French hostages the day Dietrich and his entourage arrived from Paris in a fleet of Horches and Mercedes. This time there would be no rescue attempt. The Creeper had seen to that. He had organized the execution in such a way that the old cobbled square where they were to be shot was sealed off, not only by Panzer grenadiers, but by tanks too. As for the French civilians, a ring of stern-faced 'chained dogs' and the French gendarmes who collaborated with the *Boche* kept them at a safe distance. The men who were to die were not even allowed to have a French priest administer the last rites. Instead, a tame Catholic chaplain who couldn't speak French was brought in from the Paris HQ to do the job.

Just as the high-ranking officers in their elegant uniforms, some of them with hampers of top-class food and champagne at their feet in the cars, as if this was some kind of picnic, pulled up, the hostages were led out and tied to the waiting posts. This time there would be no firing squad. Instead two trucks were driven up. They reversed swiftly and soldiers threw back their canvas hoods to reveal the two machine guns, already manned by serious-looking middle-aged 'chained dogs', waiting there. For a couple of minutes the Creeper allowed the weak-faced priest in field-grey uniform to say the prayers in German, then he ordered roughly, 'All right, enough of that mumbo-jumbo – move away, padre.'

The priest needed no urging. He moved back quickly, hiding his breviary, as if it were a book of pornography,

112

and retired behind the firing squad, his forehead glistening with sweat.

The ten, mostly middle-aged Frenchmen (for the young had already gone into hiding when they heard the rumour that the *Boche* were taking hostages) faced up to death bravely enough. A couple of them broke down and began wailing, trying to kneel and beg for mercy. But the Germans took no notice, especially the 'chained dogs' behind the machine guns; they had done this sort of thing often enough in Russia. They were used to killing defenceless people. As for the staff officers still seated in their splendid cars, taking cautious nips of cognac from their silver flasks, they seemed to be enjoying the spectacle. They appeared to be amused, especially when one of the middle-aged Frenchmen pleading for mercy wet himself in his abject fear and they nudged each other, pointing at the growing damp patch on the front of the unfortunate man's trousers.

Von Dodenburg, on his way to report as ordered to Dietrich, held up by the outer circle of 'chained dogs', frowned. He didn't like that sort of thing one bit. Senior German officers, especially in the SS, shouldn't behave in such a manner. But he realized there was nothing he could do about it. So he waited for the inevitable to happen. It didn't take long. Someone barked an order. The 'chained dogs' squinted down the long air-cooled barrels of their MG42s. Next moment they pressed their triggers in unison.

The crowd was expecting it, but that sudden burst of fire still caught them by surprise. There were gasps, cries, as the two military policemen continued firing, sweeping to left and right so that no one would be missed. The hostages twitched and jumped in a kind of frenetic dance of death, while some of the elegant staff officers held their hands to their ears, as if they couldn't stand that murderous noise.

Von Dodenburg's frown deepened ever more. He cursed violently under his breath in the same instant that he realized someone was watching him. He turned. It was Nurse Bogex,

113

a hat pulled down deep over her brow, as if she wished to conceal her beautiful face, but the handkerchief with which she was dabbing her eyes told him everything. She was sorrowing for her fellow countrymen who were being so cruelly shot.

His heart went out to her. Despite the hard looks of the 'chained dogs' facing in towards the crowd of silent French people, he touched his hand to his cap in salute and bowed slightly.

She, too, wasn't frightened of the reaction of the others. She inclined her head and gave him a wan smile.

That was encouragement enough for von Dodenburg. He knew he had to demonstrate his feelings for her whatever the police and the French thought. He started to push his way through the latter. They made way for him instantly, as if his black SS panzer uniform signified he had some sort of terrible contagious disease.

Their hands touched momentarily. But she withdrew hers almost instantly, as he whispered in French, 'I am sorry.' She replied in a whisper too, but in German: '*Ich verstehe.*' That brief exchange of words seemed to von Dodenburg later to say everything and as he turned and went on his way to meet Dietrich he felt she understood. He hoped she did, for he was moved and wished fervently that she realized that all Germans were not like the ones who had ordered these unnecessary killings which would achieve nothing but the creation of more hate and, in due course, more killing.

Sepp Dietrich was his usual swaggering, confident Bavarian self, helped perhaps by the fact he had already consumed his usual half bottle of schnapps before ten in the morning. His brown eyes twinkled merrily and he stuck out his cleft bully-boy's chin aggressively, as he greeted von Dodenburg with, 'Well, Kuno, *alter Junge*, you seem to have gotten yourself into trouble again. *Typisch.* You've been yourself again, arrogant swine that you are.'

Von Dodenburg bowed stiffly from the waist. He knew Dietrich of old. He knew, too, that the general was always like this, especially when he was half seas over, which he was now. But who had briefed Dietrich, his old divisional commander when he had been in the 'Bodyguard Division', to talk to him like this? Perhaps Witt, with the aid of the Creeper, who was standing at the edge of the group of *Prominez*, bowing and scraping and rubbing his bony fingers together like a greasy waiter in the expectation of a fat tip.

'What kind of trouble, General?' he enquired mildly.

'The usual. Feeling you know better than anyone else. Disobeying orders.' Dietrich winked knowingly. 'It appears, too, that you have been associating with a Froggie nurse, which really isn't done at your rank. Mind you –' his grin broadened – 'I do find these French girls are a damned sight more exciting than our German Hausfrauen, what.'

The Creeper, von Dodenburg told himself. Aloud he said, 'I really wouldn't know, General. I haven't your experience in such matters of – er – the heart.'

Dietrich gave him a hefty nudge with his powerful shoulder. 'There you go again, being the usual arrogant swine you are.' He took von Dodenburg by the arm and whispered out of the side of his mouth as he led von Dodenburg to the big open French window and the terrace beyond. 'Keep smiling . . . keep smiling . . . Now you talked to Rommel, didn't you?'

For a moment von Dodenburg was caught completely off guard. He gasped with shock. 'Rommel?'

'For God's sake, man, keep smiling. At Canaris's office,' he meant Santa Claus's HQ in the Tirpitzufer. 'Come on, spit it out. What do you think?'

'I don't exactly know, sir,' he managed to stutter.

'Don't know.' Dietrich dug his bruiser's fingers painfully into von Dodenburg's wounded arm. 'You're a colonel in the SS. You should damn well know!' he exclaimed angrily. 'The time has to come to piss or get off the pot. It can be a matter of days only now before they come and we act. All of us concerned want to know urgently where we stand. Are you with us or against us, Kuno?'

For a moment or two von Dodenburg's mind refused to work. Here was one of the most senior SS officers, a personal friend of Hitler's since the first days of the Nazi Party in Munich, an SS commander who had fought on every front since 1940, asking him whether he would throw in his lot with the traitors and possible assassins. It was almost impossible to comprehend a complete *volte face* of that kind.

'But what are the facts, General? How far have you got? I need to know more.'

Dietrich obviously had difficulty controlling himself. '*Facts!*' he snorted. 'When have soldiers ever been interested in facts? If they did know them, they'd never go into action. The facts would tell them that one of the pieces of shit flying around the battlefield would have their number on it sooner or later. We know what has to be done to save what we can of Germany before it's too late. That's facts enough for me, Kuno – and it should be for you, too. Now come on, man, what's it going to be?'

Miserably Kuno von Dodenburg replied, 'I don't really know, General. All I know is that I've got to do my best by the men under my command here.'

Dietrich's brown eyes blazed, but even the fiery-tempered general knew he couldn't change von Dodenburg's mind once he'd made it up. 'Then play with your little boys, *Obersturmbannführer*. But you must realize you've now cut yourself off from us – and them.' He indicated Witt, the Creeper and the rest of the officers of the Hitler Youth Division. 'And you know what happens to anyone who falls between stools? He gets a nasty pain in the arse. All right, you can go now. I won't shake your hand,' he sneered suddenly, barely able to contain his rage. 'I'm afraid my old paw is too dirty for your lily-white aristocratic hand . . .'

Outside, the crowd was breaking up. Here and there some of the French looked at the lone SS officer with eyes that burned with hatred, but most of the civilians departed with their shoulders bent, gaze on the ground, like humble folk who knew they had been defeated ever since the day they had been born.

Aimlessly von Dodenburg wandered across the square, where fatigue men were throwing down buckets of water to remove the bloodstains from the cobbles. Automatically he returned their salutes, hardly aware he was doing so. He became aware of a faint drone above him. Instinctively he looked upwards at the bright, blue June sky. For a moment or two he could see nothing. Then he spotted it – the faint white vapour trail of a plane flying very high. He knew at once what it was. 'Tommy reconnaissance plane,' he said half aloud, talking to himself in the manner of lonely men.

'Yer right there, sir,' a well-known voice agreed. It was Schulze. Again he had appointed himself the CO's unofficial bodyguard for the day. Schulze had told himself that there might be trouble with the French on this day of execution.

'It won't be long now, sir.'

Von Dodenburg knew what the big NCO meant by 'it'. The invasion. 'Yes,' he agreed, 'it won't be long now.'

They walked the rest of the way to von Dodenburg's car in silence, each man sunk in his own thoughts. Above them the lone enemy plane continued to drone round in circle after circle.

Three

Later Sergeant Schulze would remark that he never could identify what had woken him on that Tuesday, 6th June 1944. Had it been the damned 'kitchen bulls' rattling the breakfast dixies in the cookhouse, or the Frogs trundling in from the surrounding countryside in their horse-drawn carts to sell their produce on the daily market? 'All I remember,' he would remember ruefully, 'I had one helluva horn on and thought I'd better take a piss. And do you know what I saw, comrades, as I stepped outside to go to the thunderbox? No? Well, I'll tell yer for nothing. There was this Tommy floating down as large as life attached to a bit o' knicker silk. A frigging parachutist, in other words, having the frigging cheek to land on Senior Sergeant Schulze's doorstep, even before he'd had his first canteen of nigger sweat.'* Even years later when he had long become a civilian, namely a bouncer at the Hamburg Eros Zentrum, he would shake his greying head at such brazen audacity.

'And what did you do then, Sarge?' his listeners would ask though they already knew exactly what 'Senior Sergeant Schulze' had done; he had told his account of the Great Invasion numerous times before.

'What did I do? I tucked my tail back in me drawers and ran for it, toot sweet. You wasn't gonna catch me tackling the whole shitting Tommy army, was yer?'

For in that same instant that Schulze 'tucked his tail' back

*SS slang for coffee. *Transl.*

in his underpants, the dawn sky seemed to fill with British paras of the 6th Airborne, while further out at sea, as if some invisible hand had thrown a gigantic power switch, a tremendous flash of scarlet flame split the pre-dawn greyness. It was the signal for the Allied bombardment of the German coastal positions. Guns of all calibres opened up. Huge naval guns roared. Shells carrying a ton of high explosives slammed into the shore, making the very earth quiver and tremble. Shipborne mortars howled. Rocket batteries shrieked, sending battery after battery of angry missiles through the air, trailing angry red flames behind them. Red, white and green tracer zipped across the suddenly glowing water, as the God of War drew his first terrifying breath.

'*BLÜCHER! . . . BLÜCHER!*'* The code word for the start of the invasion flashed from unit to unit of the 'Baby Division'. To their front the cannon fodder of the infantry battalions of the coastal defences waited for the first landing barges to appear from the fog of war. Now they wept and cowered in their trenches, bunkers, underground chambers as they were subjected to that hellish bombardment. For four years now ever since the Tommies had been thrown out of Europe at Dunkirk they had been training for this day: to give the Tommies a reception so terrifying that the survivors of the first waves would turn tail and run to their boats in panic. But the defenders had not reckoned with such a tremendous bombardment from air and sea. They quailed.

Not the eager young volunteers of the Hitler Youth. Now as the code word flashed from unit to unit and the teenaged boys in their black and grey uniforms seized their weapons and ran to their vehicles, their motors already roaring into

---

*Field Marshal Blücher, the Prussian general of the Napoleonic wars, who thought the capital of his ally, London, would be a 'tremendous place to plunder'. In German the name is used to describe dash and daring in the phrase '*Ran wie Blücher*' – 'Up and at them like Blücher'. *Transl.*

hectic life, they threw their hats into the air with joy. They slapped each other on the back. They cheered. 'Death to the English,' they yelled exuberantly as Messerschmitts flew over at zero feet, their prop washes flushing the eager young faces turned upwards to view the sight.

'Holy strawsack!' Schulze exclaimed, stuffing stick grenades down the sides of his jackboots and wrapping great heavy belts of machine-gun ammunition around his massive shoulders. 'You'd think they were going on a frigging school picnic!'

'Some picnic!' Matz agreed a little miserably. 'And there won't be too many of the poor young shits coming back.'

'All right,' von Dodenburg butted in, as he strapped his camouflaged helmet on and slung his machine pistol over his shoulder. 'Enough doom and gloom. Get the men moving – *dalli . . . dalli.*'

'Yessir,' the two NCOs said as one. Cupping their hands around their mouths against the roar of the gunfire at the coast, they started bellowing out orders.

The teenagers obeyed eagerly. They doubled to the waiting half-tracks, which, filled with panzer grenadiers, would follow the Panther tanks, as if they couldn't get into combat swiftly enough. Von Dodenburg shook his head in mock wonder. Where would you find such boys, eager for death or some desperate glory, in the rest of the *Wehrmacht* in this, the fourth year of total war? Fools, blind fools, they might well be, but they were damned brave ones. For a moment his steely blue eyes flooded with tears at the sight of them, these boys who probably would not survive this June, and then he was businesslike again. 'Carbide,' he cried above the roar of the vehicles' engines, whose drivers gunned the motors, as if they could not get away soon enough.

Somewhere, one of the old hares started to sing the song of SS Assault Regiment Wotan. Once, it had made the Old Continent tremble with fear. Even now it sent shivers down von Dodenburg's spine. As he swung himself on to the turret of the lead Panther, he found himself singing it as well. Everywhere the old hares and the teenage greenbeaks took up the hard, harsh words of the old regiment's marching song.

> *'Clear the streets, the SS marches.*
> *The storm-columns stand at the ready.*
> *They will take the road*
> *From tyranny to freedom.*
> *So we are ready to give our all,*
> *As did our fathers before us.*
> *Let death be our companion.*
> *We are the Black Band*
> *W . . . O . . . T . . . A . . . N!'*

Then they were gone . . .

By the flickering light of the bombardment, which was still confined to the coast and the immediate hinterland, von Dodenburg studied the terrain. By now he and his men knew it well. Now he scoured it from left to right in an attempt to ascertain if any changes had been made which would indicate that the enemy was already in position, waiting for him and his tanks to roll into a trap. But even as he studied the terrain, he knew he was already disobeying orders.

The command from Panzer Group Headquarters West had been for him to make contact with the hard-pressed 719th Infantry Division, which was still holding the line of the coast. On his way to make contact he was to be on the lookout for any possible enemy airborne landing in the Hitler Youth Division's area. It was on that second part of the Panzer Group order that he was concentrating. For in the hard-bitten way of a battle-experienced commander he had already written the 719th Infantry Division off. It would be only a matter of hours before it was wiped out. In his opinion, an airborne landing in the very area in which he had trained his men was a very likely possibility and that landing would come soon.

Von Dodenburg reasoned further that once he was engaged against lightly armed paratroopers, Witt wouldn't be able to pull him out of the battle swiftly and his casualties would be lower than otherwise; for to all intents and purposes his armour would give him superiority over an even larger force of paras.

'Sir.' It was his gunner, a young corporal whose name he couldn't remember. The boy's voice was tense and low, but he was in control of himself alright.

'Where's the fire, Corporal?'

'Bush at ten o'clock,' the boy replied, using correct if very formal procedure.

'Got it!'

'There's something moving there, sir.'

Hastily von Dodenburg focused his glasses.

He spotted it almost immediately. Someone had dug a hasty slit trench inside the bush but had neglected to hide the spoil. Now in the dawn light the brown earth was clearly visible against the bright green of the bush and the surrounding grass. Carefully von Dodenburg put his glasses down and considered. Had some lone Tommy dug himself in there, albeit carelessly, revealing his position like that, or was he part of a well-concealed defensive line tempting some foolish Germans into entering a trap?

Von Dodenburg knew there was no time left to consider. He had to make a decision – *now* – even if it was going to be a tricky one. He did it. He touched his throat mike. 'Panzer 400 to Panzer 401.' He spoke rapidly to the Panther on his left flank, the one closest to the slit trench. Hastily he filled in the young corporal in charge of the big tank before warning him, 'Be on the lookout for enemy anti-tank weapons. In like Uncle Otto and at top speed. *Hals und Beinbruch.* Over and out.' The throat mike went dead.

Swiftly the unseen driver of the tank engaged the first of his many gears. A puff of white smoke from the exhausts. A rattle of tracks. A shower of dirt and stones. The Panther started to lumber forward, its long overhanging cannon swinging from side to side warily like the snout of some predatory monster seeking out its prey. Von Dodenburg crossed his fingers hastily, while his own gunner slipped a high-explosive shell into the breech of his gun. Then they watched as the big tank lumbered forward up the slight rise to the bush and the unknown which lay behind it.

The seconds passed leadenly. To the west the tremendous bombardment continued. The sky was an angry flame-red. Every now and again, fighter planes circled, black hawks against that red, dropping their bombs on the hard-pressed men of the 719th Division. Even as he watched, breath held tense von Dodenburg knew that it wouldn't be long before the 719th collapsed completely and the first wary khaki-clad infantry and cautious tanks of the British invaders started advancing into view, ready to give battle to his old hares and boys of the 'Baby Division'.

Now the other tank had almost reached within a hundred metres of the slit trench. Still there was no sign of life there. Indeed, oblivious of the fierce bombardment of the coast, the birds were flitting to and fro and in the taller trees to both sides the rooks cawed away monotonously.

Suddenly, startlingly, it happened, as von Dodenburg had half expected it would. The Panther had ridden up a slight rise, exposing its poorly armoured underbelly when, with an angry hiss, a solid white shape hurtled towards the German tank. 'AP!' the gunner yelled.

It was. An armour-piercing shell zipped across, bringing with it its message of death, right for that soft underbelly. At that range the enemy gunner couldn't miss. Steel struck steel with a great hollow boom. The Panther reeled, as if punched by a giant fist. For a moment it simply came to a stop. Nothing appeared to be happening. Abruptly from inside the tank, its engine still ticking away, there came a muffled explosion. What looked like a great smoke ring from a huge cigar rose silently from the open hatch. Next moment the 45-ton tank disintegrated. Its turret flew into the sky and landed with a great thud on the turf; steel slivers, gleaming a dull red, hissed lethally through the shattered frame, and even as the gunner yelled, 'There's more of the Tommy bastards, sir. Paras!' von Dodenburg knew that this was it: the Battle for France had commenced.

Four

'Crap, said the Lord and ten thousand subjects bent and took the strain. For in them days the word of the Lord was law,' Schulze declaimed and, bending down, placed another dead body in the ditch. He breathed out hard, spat on his meaty palms and prepared to lift another of the crudely butchered corpses. 'What a frigging life!'

Von Dodenburg pushed his helmet to the back of his cropped blond head and with the back of his sleeve wiped the sweat from his forehead. 'What a frigging life indeed,' he said to himself. They had attacked the line of the English paratroopers for nearly two hours. At the cost of some twelve deaths and two knocked-out Panthers, both still smoking on the rise, they had turfed the English out of their positions and destroyed one of their 57mm anti-tank guns. Then the English *Jabos* had come sweeping in at tree-top height, blasting the German attackers with their cannon and machine guns. Thus the Hitler Youth attack had fizzled out and the 'babies' had gone to ground. It had given the English time to pull back and occupy the next ridge line.

For the time being, the battle had petered out, save for the dry, sharp crack of a sniper's rifle and the occasional brief rattle of a machine gun. But von Dodenburg knew the lull wouldn't last. Between the two fronts lay the fields where he guessed the English gliders would land. Soon, either the English must counterattack to secure that field, or the Hitler Youth would have to do the same in order not to be swamped when the gliders came sailing in. Either way, von Dodenburg

125

told himself glumly, there were bound to be losses; and all the while the German radios were screaming HQ's demand to know why he had not yet contacted the hard-pressed 719th Infantry Division on the coast. Sooner or later some big shot from the Hitler Youth would arrive on this lonely battlefield to start threatening him.

Von Dodenburg spat drily and wondered what he should do while he still had a chance to make independent decisions. He stared down at the line of English dead in the ditch, their faces green with strange blotches of yellow and green. No one had bothered to close their eyes. Now they seemed to leer at him, their mouths crumpled and gaping, lips drawn back to reveal their teeth, like wild animals snarling their last defiance. He took his gaze away from the faces hastily. His eyes fell on the brown boots of the officers, contrasting with the black ones of the other ranks. He smiled slightly despite his gloomy mood. Even in death, the English officer and his troops appeared to be separated by class. Strange.

'Air alarm, sir!' One of the old hares cut into his thoughts. 'To the west.'

Von Dodenburg reacted at once. He swung round, raising his glasses as he did so. Behind him the soldiers fell on their backs and aimed their rifles, while the machine gunners tilted their MG42s to their fullest extent. It was obvious that they expected another air attack.

Von Dodenburg wasn't so sure. The 'Vs' of attacking planes, just vague black dots on the blue horizon at the moment, seemed to him to be moving too slowly for fighter-bombers. He adjusted his focus. Now he could make out the tugs, two-engined obsolete bombers, each towing two other planes, both without engines. He knew what that meant. The gliders were on their way, bringing up the reinforcements for the Tommy paras already on the ground and there seemed to be a damned lot of them.

Von Dodenburg didn't hesitate. 'Gliders,' he alerted his men. Those who were resting swung round and faced the field to their front; those under Schulze, bringing in the bloody corpses, dropped them and doubled back to their positions at top speed.

It was now that the green signal flares started to sail into the sky from the British positions, some hundred metres away. Von Dodenburg knew what that meant. The paras had spotted the gliders approaching too or were in radio contact with them. It meant that they would have to recapture the DZ or defend it strongly enough to prevent the Germans from doing so.

Von Dodenburg shouted to Schulze as the drone of massed aircraft engines became ever louder. 'To me, Schulze, at the double!'

Despite his bulk, the big sergeant moved with surprising speed. He slammed into the ditch next to the CO and gasped, 'They're going to attempt to land over there, sir?'

'Exactly . . . and we're going to stop them.'

'Naturally we are, sir,' Schulze replied with a big grin, as if it were the most natural thing in the world that an SS combat command could beat what von Dodenburg later found out was a whole brigade of some 3,000 gliderborne infantry. 'What's the drill?'

'You take the infantry.'

'Infantry! You call them teenage titty-suckers infantry—' Schulze began to sneer. But von Dodenburg cut him off with, 'This afternoon, Schulze, we're going to wean those babies off the tit. Today we make soldiers of them. Now as I was saying . . .'

Over the coast the last of the surviving German anti-aircraft guns took on the glider fleet that was passing over the guns in majestic slowness. The sky filled with white tracer, fiery red sparks trailing behind it. Brown puffballs of exploding flak appeared on all sides. Here and there a glider was hit and started to descend in slow, winding circles, trailing smoke behind it. The rest sailed on with inexorable purpose, as if nothing could stop the airborne armada; while in the paras' lines, the whistles shrilled, the hunting horns sounded and NCOs cursed angrily. The paras were about to attack and recapture the field before the Germans did. Now it was a race against time. The fate of the invasion lay in the hands of these handfuls of desperate men, German and English . . .

But by now others were beginning to play a role in the outcome of the battle soon to come. As the hollow roaring of scores of planes drowned even the thunder of the barrage, the gliders came flying by: great boxlike structures of canvas and wood, being towed by planes that couldn't even attempt to dodge the flak and the lethal Morse of tracer hurrying to meet them.

The men on the ground, German and Canadian, had no eyes for the airborne armada, however. The fight for the little French hamlet was too intense. For both sides had bumped into each other without any chance of preparing a plan of attack. The Canadians had found a hole in the 719th Division's front. They hadn't hesitated. They had seized this golden opportunity without even notifying their HQ what they were going to do. The column of Sherman tanks with the infantry on their decks had raced on up the dead-straight country road that led to Montgomery's primary D-Day objective – Caen. And then they had hit the Hitler Youth reconnaissance party head on.

The Creeper, who had been made the commander of this hastily thrown together party of panzer grenadiers in their half-tracks and a handful of Panthers, had been frightened out of his wits as the first armour-piercing shell had slammed into the lead half-track. It had come to an abrupt stop, its left track rolling out behind it like a severed metal limb. Hastily the young grenadiers had baled out of the stricken vehicle to left and right as they had been taught to do. But the Canadians, rough, tough backwoodsmen for the most part, weren't playing the game as the Hitler Youth had been informed they would. They didn't give the greenhorns the chance to find cover. For their machine-gunners had opened up immediately. They mowed the fleeing men down mercilessly. Within a matter of seconds, or so it seemed to a horrified, ashen-faced Creeper, a good dozen Hitler Youth were dying, moaning for their mothers, in the road that ran with blood.

That had been the bloody start of the battle for this nameless hamlet. And so it now continued as the gliders began to release their tows and started to come down in an uncanny silence. Time and time again, each side tried to rush and take the village. More than once it came to hand-to-hand fighting in which no quarter was given or expected. The Germans and the Canadians hacked, stabbed, tore at each other like primitive animals, cursing and gasping, eyes wide and wild with hate and fear.

The Creeper, for his part, sheltered in his quickly established 'command post' underneath a stout Norman kitchen table, with heavy wooden boxes placed on it for extra protection, his distended nostrils filled with the smell of garlic, unwashed bodies and the sourness of hard work. Not that he noticed. He was too frightened to do anything but pray that the Canadians wouldn't find him when they took his 'CP'.

Fortunately for him they didn't. A resourceful old hare took over the remaining three Panthers, although he was only a simple soldier, reduced to the rank of ordinary private more than once in his long career with the SS. 'Come on, you frigging heroes,' he rallied the scared young tankers, 'do you want to live for frigging ever!' He took a hefty swig from his flatman, wiped his sleeve across his unshaven chin and sprang on the lead tank. '*Los*, let's show them Tommies in their pisspot helmets what real soldiers are like! . . . CARBIDE!'

Scared at that moment more by the unshaven old hare than the Canadians, who were now trying to outflank the burning village, the three tank drivers obeyed the order. Engines going all out, they ploughed through the fields to the right flank, snapping down trees as if they were matchwood, throwing up huge wakes of grass sods and black earth, while, perched on the turret of the first Panther, the old hare laughed crazily as if this was the greatest joke in the world.

They caught the attacking Canadian Shermans completely by surprise. The Canadians had been too sure; they had thought they had these callow German kids on the run. So it was that as the line of Canadian tanks rode out of the village street towards the fields, the three Panthers were waiting for them behind a rough stone wall in the hulldown position. What happened next wasn't a battle; it was a massacre.

One after another the Shermans were hit at close range by the Panthers' great overhanging 75mm cannon. The German shells slammed into them mercilessly. The Canadians didn't stand a chance. While the lone old hare sat on his metal perch, crying above the flame and thunder of the tank battle, 'Stick it up 'em! . . . Try that on for collar size, you Tommy buck-teeth bastards!', his young gunners knocked out seven Shermans within so many minutes. It was too much for the Canadians, as hard and as tough as they were: while the remaining two tanks turned and fled, firing smoke as they did so, the survivors trying to escape were mown down without mercy by the flushed, triumphant Hitler Youth. They had been brought up ever since they had been kids in the short black pants of the Hitler Youth Movement to be 'hard as Krupp steel'. Now they showed just how hard they were.

To no avail some of the Candians threw up their arms in surrender, crying, '*Kamerad!*' But their plea for mercy went unanswered. The tank machine guns swept the field, the tracer hissing in a white fury over the cropped, churned grass, sweeping the fleeing Canadians away as if they were puny insignificant creatures of no value. In a few minutes it was all over. Still the gunners, carried away by the crazy atavistic blood fury of battle, continued to fire their machine guns until the old hare, weary of the slaughter, yelled, 'Cease fire . . .

cease fire, you crazy young arseholes. They're dead . . . Do you understand, *the poor shits are dead*!'

Five minutes later, a patrol of flushed, triumphant panzer grenadiers, the pockets of their camouflaged smocks filled and bulging with looted Canadian chocolate, reported to the Creeper as he emerged from his hiding place, 'They've gone, sir – the Tommies have done a bunk. But . . .' They hesitated and their spokesman, the leader of the patrol, lowered his gaze, as if abruptly embarrassed. 'But they've left . . . left something behind, sir,' he stammered.

'What do you mean – left something behind?' the Creeper snapped sternly, as if he were back at the *Realschule* faced by some reluctant, ill-prepared pupil. 'Out with it, soldier!'

But even now the young patrol leader couldn't quite bring himself to relate what he had discovered, that terrible thing, while the others had been busy, joyously looting the Canadian dead of their chocolate and cigarettes. Instead, he mumbled, 'I think it's best, sir, if you come and have a look for yourself.' He lowered his gaze again.

The Creeper gave in. 'All right, I suppose I have to do everything.' Muttering that, 'I don't think you men realize the many responsibilities of a commanding officer during a battle,' he followed the patrol out into the suddenly silent village, the air heavy with a strange brooding tension.

Five

The first flight of gliders came swooping in silently, the only sound they made the hiss of the wind under their big wings. Von Dodenburg licked his parched lips. He hadn't had a drink since they had first been alerted for action, but it wasn't thirst that made him so dry; it was a kind of fear. What could his force – a handful of old hares and some couple of hundred greenbeaks do against such a mighty air armada?

For above him the tugs were releasing glider after glider, circling slowly, as below them the dug-in English paras continued to fire their signal flares into the bright June sky. An hour before, he and his men had made an attempt to capture the landing site. Their attack had been bold and resolute. But it had failed. The paras had fought back with iron determination. In the end von Dodenburg had been forced to order the retreat to their original positions before he lost any more men. Now the field for which the gliders were heading was littered with the bodies of his young soldiers, sprawled in the extravagant postures of those done violently to death, dead before they had really begun to live.

Behind von Dodenburg, the young radio operator, his face dirty and lathered with sweat, was still trying to raise someone, his voice cracked and hoarse now after an hour of trying to contact someone who could send reinforcements. Earlier von Dodenburg had managed to contact Witt. But the fat divisional commander had been negative. 'You've got yourself into that mess, Kuno,' he had barked harshly, while the earphones crackled with the immense radio traffic going on, 'you get yourself out of it.'

'But I need reinforcements desperately,' he had pleaded urgently 'in the clear', throwing radio procedure to the winds.

Witt had shown no understanding. 'I have none, Kuno. The whole shitting front has gone up in flames. We've got to stop the main traffic. The Canadians are already within sight of Caen. Over and out!' With that the radio had gone dead. Now von Dodenburg's radio operator was trying to raise anyone, SS or *Wehrmacht*, who might have men to spare to help blast these gliderborne enemy soldiers out of the sky before they had a chance to land and reinforce the established paras.

Von Dodenburg forgot the radio. The paras had now commenced firing tracer at the poles which were supposed to prevent gliders landing on the fields between the two fronts. He knew why. They hoped to set them alight before the gliders touched down and crashed into them. But he realized almost immediately that whoever was commanding this operation was not worried about crash landings; they were going to come down whether there was danger awaiting them or not.

The time had come to act. He rose to his feet boldly. Ten metres away in his trench with Matz, Schulze called urgently, 'Get down for Chrissake, sir!' Von Dodenburg didn't seem to hear. He shouted as the first gliders came lower and lower, 'Stand to . . . stand to . . . Fire at the cockpits and the doors . . . don't waste ammo on the fuselage . . . STAND TO!'

His men tensed. They raised their weapons. Schulze spat on his hands, as if he might be about to engage in a fist fight, and cried to no one in particular, 'Now try this on for frigging collar size!' He raised his machine pistol, which looked like a child's toy in his big paws, and aimed.

The ground raced to meet the gliders. The pilots ignored the tracer coming their way from the German position. They concentrated totally on bringing the flimsy craft down in one piece and discharging their human cargo swiftly. For, above them, scores of gliders were circling like silent hawks, awaiting their turn. Now they were coming in at 100 m.p.h. A glider struck one of the burning posts. Its wing was torn off. Desperately the pilot tried to keep control. To no avail. The glider swerved violently. Next moment it hit the ground with a violent thud, turned on its side and disintegrated. No one got out.

Still the other pilots pressed on. At the very last moment the pilots jerked the gliders' noses slightly upwards and pressed the brake flaps. Next instant the first of the wooden planes – two thousand pounds of men and material – slammed to the ground. Grinding and rending canvas and wood, the engineless planes slid across the fields, trailing a great wake of earth behind them, the barbed wire wrapped around the gliders' skids to shorten the sliding distance, snapping like string. Then, with one last mighty heave, the first of the planes lurched to a stop and the SS started peppering the door and the nose with fire, waiting for their victims to emerge. The battle for the landing zone had commenced . . .

The Creeper wanted to vomit. In all his wildest dreams he had never imagined anything like this – and by nature he was one of those men whose mild exterior concealed a sadistic longing. Everything, the cries of rage, the noise of battle, the drone of the enemy bombers heading for Caen, faded into the distance so that he might as well have been deaf, as his eyes behind his pince-nez took in the full horror of the scene.

A young Hitler Youth grenadier hung from one of those concrete telegraph poles typical of France. His tormentors had thought to play a macabre joke on the dead grenadier. They had twisted a piece of rusty barbed wire into shape and hung it around the hanging, bloody head like a wreath of thorns and, to complete the 'crucifixion', the retreating Canadians had removed his boots and scored his feet a bright red with their bayonets as they had fled.

But that wasn't all. As the Creeper's hearing returned and he became aware of his surroundings, standing as he was in the middle of the cobbled square with the dead sprawled among the debris everywhere, someone cried in shocked horror, 'God in heaven, do you see what they've done . . . to his flies . . .' The youth who had cried couldn't finish his sentence. Overcome totally, he turned and began to vomit in the gutter, his skinny shoulders heaving mightily like those of a broken-hearted child.

The Creeper fought back the desire to vomit himself by an effort of sheer willpower. The Canadians had not only crucified the dead soldier, they had emasculated him too. On the ground at his bloody, tortured feet, his penis lay in the dust like a grey shrivelled worm. 'Holy God,' the Creeper heard himself cry, *'was für eine Schweinerei'* – *what an awful piggery* – 'How could men do such a thing—?' He broke off.

Enemy artillery was now beginning to range in on the village abandoned by the defeated Canadians only an hour before. Ranging shells, which gave off yellow smoke for better observation, were falling in the fields to the west of the place. Soon they'd do the same to the east. When the range had been established, they'd plaster the village itself. The Creeper realized that things were becoming dangerous again and the former schoolmaster was a man who had a passionate interest in avoiding danger. It was time to go. Still, the Canadian atrocity couldn't go unpunished.

'Bring the prisoners out,' he ordered. Now he was very masterful, feeling more control than ever; indeed it was like being back at the *Realschule* when he had held sway over thirty frightened fourteen-year-olds. 'Immediately. They will pay the price for this bloody business.'

His teenage soldiers were only too eager to carry out his orders. They wanted revenge, too, however terrible that revenge might be.

Moments later they were shoving eight Canadians in front

of them roughly, including two wounded, one of whom was so badly hit that he was having to crawl on his bloody hands and knees on to the street.

There was an angry murmur from the rest of the Hitler Youth outside when they saw the Canadians. Someone cried, 'Let me get my paws on the murdering swine. I'll cut their nuts off with a broken beer bottle.'

'Enough of that,' the Creeper snapped, totally in charge now, transformed by events from the trembling coward to the masterful man of action. 'We're not barbarians like they are. We Germans do not torture our prisoners. They shall be punished, but they will be punished cleanly in accordance with the high moral code of the SS.'

Somehow the Canadians seemed to have understood his words. They realized that they were going to be shot. Perhaps they were first-generation Canadians of German stock – there were plenty of those in Canada's all-volunteer army. They started to plead with the teenage SS, two of them in broken German, wringing their hands in the classical pose of supplication, begging, 'Don't shoot us . . . we were your prisoners . . . We couldn't have done that – thing . . .' – all save the man who had been forced to crawl into the battle-littered street on his hands and knees.

He sat down now, gasping a little with pain, but his bloody face bearing a look of angry defiance. 'Knock it off,' he snarled. 'You don't want to have no truck with the Krauts, fellas. You're Canucks, be proud—' He never finished his sentence. With a cool precision and deliberation that surprised himself, the Creeper pulled out his pistol, hardly aimed and with a slight grimace fired straight at the defiant Canadian's face.

At that range the Creeper couldn't miss. The slug caught the Canadian squarely in the centre of his face. It seemed to disintegrate, looking as if someone had suddenly thrown a handful of red jam at it. He reeled back without even a moan, dead before he hit the cobbles.

That act of cold-blooded murder seemed to serve as a signal for the youths of the Hitlerjugend Division. Without even an order, they started firing their weapons into the terrified Canadians, while the Creeper, a cold smile on his thin, cruel lips, looked on. The Canadians hadn't a chance. Some simply took the slugs. Others held up their hands to shelter their faces as if they might ward off the hard steel. One cried, 'Oh, my God . . . help me, Lord.' But the Lord was looking the other way that hot June morning.

Five minutes later the Creeper's little reconnaissance force had retreated down that same road towards Caen, leaving the dead sprawled out there in an awkward pile, their rich red blood drip-dripping into the white, dry dust.

Perhaps it was a matter of thirty minutes or so afterwards that the first Canadian scout car of the 3rd Canadian Reconnaissance Regiment came crawling cautiously round the bend in the country road, its turret aerial whipping back and forth in the hot sunlight like a glowing steel lash. Another five after that and the car commander with his silver lightning badge of the Canadian Recce was bending over the dead, his broad, suntanned face contorted with horror, while he tried to wave away the greedy fat bluebottles which were already beginning to feed on their blood.

Inside the scout car's turret, the radio operator, who had just stopped vomiting after seeing the man hanging from the pole in mock crucifixion, was saying thickly, 'Hello, Sunray . . . Hello, Sunray . . . Want to report an atrocity . . . Our men murdered in cold blood . . . Hello, Sunray . . .'

A little later 'Sunray', the CO of the Canadian Reconnaissance Regiment, was reporting, in his turn, to the brigade commander, 'Sir, the Krauts have turned vicious. Reports are coming in of various atrocities being committed on our prisoners . . . They're shooting our guys out of hand . . . What are we going to do about it?'

It was a question that would not receive an official answer; that would be too dangerous if such an order was committed to paper. But as the news swept through the rank and file of the advancing Canadians, the mood of the ordinary soldiers turned nasty and ugly. The troops might not have heard of the Geneva Convention. But from now onwards, they certainly weren't going to observe it, or any of the rules of warfare when prisoners were taken. From now onwards the battle between the Canadian 3rd Infantry Division and the 'Baby Division' was to be a very personal matter. Both sides had already become brutalized. Prisoners on both sides were now at the mercy of their captors. A wrong word, a look of defiance, a simple gesture even, could easily turn into sudden death, cold-blooded murder.

Six

Now it was almost evening. Still the battle for the landing strip continued. Twice von Dodenburg's little force had beaten off determined attacks by the gliderborne troops, who obviously wanted to clear the place of the Germans so that they could bring in their heavy equipment, jeeps, anti-tank cannon, small engineering structures and the like; and twice von Dodenburg had beaten them off. But while the German force was growing progressively smaller due to casualties, the glidermen were growing in numbers as the troop gliders kept sailing in, bringing in ever more reinforcements.

Grimly von Dodenburg stared at the lunar landscape of battle, wondering if he still might beat the Tommies. To his left another shattered glider had burst into flames, casting its lurid light on the dead who lay everywhere. To his front a wrecked cannon slumped on one side, its dead strewn around it, blown to pieces by the shell from his one remaining Panther, which had scored a direct hit on the gun. Now its crew looked like the bloody pieces of offal he remembered seeing outside butchers' shops before the war. He frowned. One never got used to the real cost of combat in human life, he told himself. Veteran as he was, he was always shocked anew by the sight of a battlefield after the battle was over.

Over the Tommies' lines the green flares were sailing into the darkening sky once more. Obviously another serial of gliders was coming in. Next to him, Schulze, who was smoking one of the Capstan cigarettes he had taken off a dead para (though he had complained, 'Don't those buck-teethed

139

Tommies drink anything but frigging tea? I haven't found a single drop of booze on 'em yet'), said gloomily, 'Where in God's name do they get all them gliders? There's no end to the shitting things.'

Von Dodenburg didn't reply. He was thinking too hard. Now he was convinced he could no longer break through the Tommies' line with the men still available to him; and he knew once darkness fell the enemy would attack in strength, and that would be the end of that. He wouldn't be able to hold them. Still there might yet be a way to throw a spanner in the works and get them so disorganized that they would have to postpone the final attack. Then with luck, Witt might have found him some reinforcements to bolster up his eggshell-thin line.

'Schulze –' he turned to the big noncom – 'what about the Panther?' He referred to his last runner, the remaining tank capable of movement. 'We've got fuel.'

'Enough, sir,' Schulze answered without much interest. For he knew once the Panther broke out of its camouflaged pit and tried to make a run for it, the Tommies would concentrate every available anti-tank weapon on the tank. It wouldn't even reach the road behind the Hitlerjugend's positions.

'Ammo?'

'Plenty.'

Matz, lolling in the trench next to the other two, said, 'Won't stand much of a chance, backing out with that monster, sir.'

Von Dodenburg forced a laugh, but it was strained. 'We're not going to be backing out, Matz,' he answered. 'We're going forward!'

Matz whistled softly through his teeth and cursed, '*Scheisse!*'

Schulze, for his part, folded his big dirty paws as if in prayer and said piously, 'For what we are about to receive may the good Lord make us thankful . . .'

The big tank burst out of its camouflaged pit as the last serial of gliders began landing some 250 metres away. With a roar that startled even the weary Hitler Youth teenagers crouching half-asleep in their foxholes, it burst through the hedge and into the fields beyond, Schulze, next to von Dodenburg in the turret, firing smoke to both sides, while Matz below in the driver's cramped chamber thrust home gear after gear, knowing that he'd better obtain top speed as soon as possible, or else.

But for the moment the lone German tank had achieved surprise. Spraying grass and wet, marshy clay to both sides, it rolled straight towards the approaching gliders with barely a single shot being fired at it. Once a lone para, armed with a clumsy PIAT, the British anti-tank projector, stood and was about to fire at the Panther. Schulze didn't give him a chance. He pressed the trigger of the turret machine gun. It burst into frenetic life. Tracer zipped towards the lone soldier. Suddenly what appeared to be a series of red buttonholes was stitched across his chest. He screamed in agony. Arms flailing, he disappeared beneath the tracks of the racing Panther to be pulped by the cruel tracks. 'Should have got out of the frigging way,' Schulze commented unfeelingly.

Von Dondenburg said nothing. He was concentrating on the gliders racing towards them on a collision course. He knew the Panther wouldn't survive more than a few more minutes. But before the Tommies ranged in on the tank, he wanted to make a mess of the glider formation.

Now as the first tracer started to bounce off the Panther's thick metal hide like glowing golfballs, the pilots tried to take wild evasive action. Schulze whooped exuberantly. He fired the last of the smoke dischargers and yelled, 'That's the stuff to give the frigging troops!' At his side in the hot, fetid turrets, peering through the narrow slit, which gave him very limited vision, Kuno grabbed hold of some support ready for what was to come. 'AT fire, two o'clock. Deploy—'

His words were drowned by the great clang of metal on metal. The Panther reared up on its rear bogies like a bucking bronco in a Western film. Suddenly the interior was full of the acrid stink of burnt cordite. Von Dodenburg said a hurried prayer. But the tough hide of the Panther survived the hit. With a crash, the front of the 46-ton tank hit the ground and was moving once more. 'Holy strawsack,' Schulze roared over the intercom, 'I nearly pissed mesen then.'

'What d'yer mean – *nearly*,' Matz below called back. 'I've got the piss pouring down my left leg like the frigging River Rhine.'

Now they were closing ever faster with the leading gliders, racing along the ground, trailing a wild wake of earth and stones behind them, as their pilots fought to maintain control. Von Dodenburg snapped out, 'Schulze, traverse right . . . up a hundred . . . Left glider.'

Hurriedly a sweating Schulze swung the great hooded 75mm cannon round, his big fingers like hairy pork sausages working the gun's elevator mechanism almost lovingly. 'On,' he rapped.

'Fire!'

The air in front of the Panther flashed a bright, blinding yellow. The ten-ton turret rocked like a shaken toy. Blast thrust back into the turret, as the spent shell case rattled to the floor. Von Dodenburg shoved in the next round, as Schulze peered through his periscope and cursed, 'Shit, sir . . . A short!'

'Up fifty,' von Dodenburg cried urgently as in front the nearest glider pilot pulled up the nose of the frail craft and narrowly missed ploughing into the steaming brown hole made by the Panther's shell.

Crazily Schulze whirled the wheel round. Next instant he pulled the firing lever. Again the turret heaved. Von Dodenburg peered through his slit. For an instant his vision was obscured by smoke. Abruptly it cleared. He whooped with joy. The nearest glider had disintegrated. Men were flying through the air, whirling their arms and legs crazily before slamming into the ground, dead. 'We got the swine!' he shouted exuberantly, as Schulze went to work spraying the wreckage in case anyone had survived the explosion. No one had.

'Look out!' Matz cried from below. 'Fire from one clock!' Almost to their immediate front, there was the violet flash of flame. For a moment they could see the solid white blur of an armour-piercing shell. Schulze fired in the same moment that Matz swung the big steel monster round. Just in time. A whooshing rush of air. The frightening backlash of a shell passing hair-close to the turret. The AP shell flew by them to bury itself harmlessly in the earth a hundred metres beyond.

Now Schulze went to work on the incoming gliders. Desperately the pilots tried to avoid the massacre to come while the Tommy anti-tank gunners sought to neutralize the lone tank. But Matz was too smart for them. He had driven the Panther into a hulldown position behind a slight rise in the ground. It was dangerous, but so far the solid shot projectiles were hissing uselessly just above the turret.

'Well done, Matz,' von Dodenburg yelled excitedly over the intercom.

'Don't bother about the tin –' he meant a medal – Matz yelled back. 'Just give me an immediate transfer so I can drive a desk in the Army Pay Corps.'

Von Dodenburg laughed and told himself once again what fine fellows his old hares were. They were coarse, even brutal, but in an emergency like this he knew he could depend upon them one hundred per cent.

But already Matz, crouched in his driving seat, was taking an active part in the one-sided battle too. From below there came the vicious high-pitched *brr-brr* of his machine gun, as he raked the running survivors of another glider which Schulze's shells had just wrecked. In a flash he had cut three of them down, while another one went to ground, feigning death. Matz knew that. He paused long enough to give the Tommy a chance to make a break for it. He did. Matz showed no mercy. He pressed his trigger. The running soldier was almost cut in two before he had gone ten metres.

'Will they never learn?' he said to no one in particular over the intercom, which was now filled with the crackling static of the battle. 'If he'd stayed there, he might have lived to tell his heroic stories to his grandkids.'

'Grandkids!' Schulze sneered. 'Who'd want grandkids for this kind o' frigging lark!'

Again the big NCO pulled the firing lever. Another glider vanished, as if it had never been there. '*Hurrah!*' Schulze cried in triumph, as von Dodenburg rammed another HE shell into the smoking breech and Matz swung the big tank round to tackle yet another glider swooping in to its doom.

But the lone Panther's advance of death and glory was about to end. Unseen by the threesome in the tank, one of the wrecked gliders had managed to discharge its cargo. Now the little tracked vehicle, pulling its trailer of liquid death and destruction behind it, came crunching its way through the wreckage and over the bodies of the dead sprawled outside the open nose. Now its driver, aware of just how vulnerable he and his vehicle were, if he were spotted before he reached his target, put his foot down – hard. He spurted forward, slamming through the gears in the brass grid, heading after the Panther.

Matz, concentrating on his front, was caught totally by surprise by the sudden whoosh. Almost immediately he felt the air being dragged from his lungs and the sudden heat which made him break out into an immediate sweat. He threw a glance to his rear. '*Grosse Scheisse!*' he cursed, feeling a sudden fear, as he recognized the vehicle chasing his tank. 'Flame-thrower!' he yelled frantically over the intercom. 'There's a frigging Tommy flame-thrower on our tail—'

His words were drowned as, with a great hiss, a stream of blue flame shot across the intervening space, charring the grass as it did so, to slap against the side of the Panther. For an instant the interior of the turret glowed a dull, evil purple colour and von Dodenburg choked, as he felt the heat swamp him, dragging the air out of him. 'Matz,' he cried in a strangled voice. 'Turn—'

But it was already too late. The flame-thrower operator in his converted Bren-gun carrier fired once more. This time that terrible flame penetrated the engine cowling. *Whoosh!* The Panther's fuel tanks went up immediately. In a flash the whole top structure of the Panther was burning furiously. What looked like the flame of some gigantic blowtorch seared the paintwork, making it bubble and burst like the symptoms of some loathsome skin disease.

Von Dodenburg didn't hesitate. They hadn't a chance now. 'Bale out . . . bale out,' he ordered frantically. 'OUT!'

The other two needed no urging. Faces contorted with abject fear, they flung themselves out of the doomed tank. Seconds later they and the rest of the little command were running for their lives. Kuno von Dodenburg had failed, and even as they ran, von Dodenburg knew there was no hope for the German side. The invasion had already virtually succeeded. From now onwards to the final end, it would be like this all the time. He and the rest of his fellow Germans would run and run until they could run no further . . .

BOOK FOUR

Endgame

Do not believe that soldiers get used to war and danger. They never do.

A. Worden

One

It was a month since von Dodenburg and his old hares had failed to dislodge the Tommies on the River Orne. Since then they had fought day in, day out, week after week, in the defence of Caen. For Montgomery's objective of D-One had still not been taken.

Now what was left of the 'Baby Division' was at the end of its tether. Dug in near Caen's garrison church, not far from divisional headquarters, the old hares and the greenbeaks who had survived so far squatted in the 'hides' amid the rubble of the shattered cathedral city, too worn, too emotionally drained to enjoy the bowl or canteen of Giddy-up Soup, their first hot food for days, which Schulze had managed to blackmail 'them thieving kitchen bulls' at headquarters to give them. They hardly moved, wordless, reddened lack-lustre eyes not even taking in the Allied reconnaissance planes circling above, surveying the ruins for yet another area of attack. Like dumb animals they waited numbly for the coming attack.

Only Schulze and Matz made an effort. Naturally their conversation was on 'Subject Number One', namely sex. Schulze was saying slowly, as if he was finding it difficult to concentrate enough to get the words out, 'She was some sort of Frog, Matzi, but did she have a milk factory in front of her? And her pearly gates.' He gave a dry whistle. 'Big and plump. You sank into her like she was made of silk cushions. If I was capable, Matzi, I'd have a hard on, just thinking o' her.'

Sadly Matz shook his head, a single tear trickling slowly

down his wizened features and dropping into his thick pea soup. 'Them days is over, Schulzi. We'll never have another hard on, old house.'

'Yer can say that again. Cut off in our prime, that's what it is. What would the Führer say, if he knew what his brave soldier boys was suffering.'

'He'd say,' Flipper, the other of these old hares who had arrived from Russia in what now seemed another life, commented, '"I'd rather fuck than fight. I'll leave that to my brave soldier boys."' He managed a wet raspberry, and the Creeper, who was making his way back to the safety of the HQ, looked at him hard. But he said nothing. He was too eager to get down to the cellars beneath the building, which was several storeys tall. Already Standartenführer Witt had been killed in the month-long battle for Caen. Officers were dying like flies; he didn't intend to be one of them. Besides, his Lore had vanished, complete with a suitcase full of those plump Westphalian sausages and hams that she gorged herself on. Now, he told himself, in that prim schoolmasterly fashion of his, he had no one else to care for; it was his duty to survive and carry on the holy creed of National Socialism. Thus he left a knowing Schulze and the rest of those disgusting people in that arrogant bastard von Dodenburg's little command to take the Führer's name in vain without comment.

For a while they slumped there in their scrapes, listening to the rumble of the permanent barrage in the distance, watching with weary, red-rimmed eyes the myriad flares sailing into the grey sky over the English lines. Von Dodenburg had seen it all before. He knew what it signified. The Tommies would be attacking soon. He knew he should alert his men, but somehow he simply didn't have the strength to crawl from one man to the other and give them the usual instructions he gave to his subordinates before an attack. It was as if an invisible tap had been opened somewhere in his body and all his usual strength and energy had been drained off. He felt old, very old. As the first big drops of the summer rain began to patter down, heralding the storm to come, he wished suddenly that it would be all over. He was sick of war – totally.

The rain started to fall in earnest about six that night. By seven it had become a steady downpour, adding to the misery of the handful of soldiers sheltering in the ruins. Someone had found a collection of potato sacks, perhaps left by the peasants, who had used them to bring their produce into the city's market. Miserably von Dodenburg crouched with the rest, his head under one of the sacks, smelling of earth and cat's pee. A couple of metres away, an equally miserable Schulze moaned, 'And now even God's pissin' on us. What's a shitting life we live.'

Von Dodenburg knew he had to do something, if even Schulze was beginning to complain. He raised his voice above the drumbeat of the rain on the ruins, 'I know it's a piggery, this rain, comrades. But look at it like this. The rain's on our side. It'll scupper the Tommy armour when they attack. Their tanks are not fitted for mud like ours are, developed as they were for the Russian winter. They'll bog down and,' he added, trying to sound more confident than he felt, 'you know we can manage the Tommy stubble-hoppers with one hand tied behind our backs. No, comrades, the rain's on our side. It'll stop the enemy armour. Their attack'll fizzle out before it even starts in this downpour, believe you me.'

Von Dodenburg knew they didn't quite believe him; they had heard too many optimistic forecasts in these last terrible weeks, but his words perked Schulze up. With new hope in his voice, he growled, 'Give me a shot o' firewater, sir, say half a litre of schnapps, and I'll tackle the tea-drinking Tommies all on my own, won't I, Matzi?'

'If you say so, Schulzi,' Corporal Matz said without conviction and then he closed his eyes, his nostrils full of the stink of the potato sacks, and tried to warm his skinny, chilled body with the memory of the time he'd had Fifi behind her own bar, with her silk knickers around her ankles, wriggling her plump little arse delightfully while he went at it like a fiddler's elbow.

But as it grew ever darker, von Dodenburg was going to be proved wrong about the rain. If anything the rain would assist the coming Allied attack . . .

'It won't be long, lads, now,' the CO of the South Staffs said, passing from soldier to soldier as they crouched in the ditch, their capes glistening with the raindrops pelting down off their helmets in wild fury.

To left and right of the start line, from whence the new boys would attack, Churchill tanks rumbled into position throwing up great clouds of mud and soil. In front of them the sappers with their mine detectors were swinging from left to right like grass-cutters back home, seeking anti-tank mines. Here and there flares still sailed into the night air, hanging there for what seemed an eternity, colouring everything below with their garish light before sliding to the earth like fallen angels.

The little General with his beaky nose and sharp blue eyes nodded his approval. All was in place for the follow-up attack. On left and right flank he had his two battle-experienced infantry divisions, the 50th and 3rd, which had been fighting since D-Day, and here in the centre he had his newest division, the 59th, which was totally green, but well trained with good sturdy soldiers from the Midlands in its ranks.

Like his soldiers, the little General stood in the pouring rain. He was carrying his green gamp, just like his great predecessor the Duke of Wellington had done a century before, but he wasn't going to open it and shelter beneath the civilian umbrella in front of these soaked young men, their boots clogged with mud as if they were soled with lead, who were now going into their first battle at dawn.

Instead he paced slowly down the lines of soldiers, their faces a white blur in the pouring rain. Behind him, although he was strictly against smoking personally, his young officers handed out green packets of Woodbines to the troops.

He paused at the Staffs' CO. The little General could just make out the sand-coloured ribbon of the Africa Star on the colonel's chest. The man seemed vaguely familiar. He'd served with him in the desert; at least he'd be battle-experienced. With luck he'd survive what was to come, but the little General had a feeling he wouldn't. He'd lead from the front. Soon he'd be dead. It was always the best, the bold, the brave who went first.

'How old are your men, Colonel?' he asked.

The young CO with the Africa Star choked back his surprise at meeting the little General so far forward; generals usually didn't venture further than brigade headquarters. 'Twenty-two, sir, is the average, sir,' he responded promptly, though, in reality, he didn't know the average age of his Midlanders.

'A good age,' the little General said thoughtfully, trying to size up the other officer in the dripping rain. 'Make the best infantry. Not that we'll really need them, fine fellows that they are. We've got something up our sleeve this time. Save their lives. We'll knock the Hun for six this time, believe you me, Colonel.'

'Yessir. Of course, sir,' the young CO answered. He didn't believe the little General. They had been trying to take Caen for over a month now. Division after division had been thrown into the bloody battle for the Norman town. Without success.

'Well, carry on, and good luck to you and your chaps.' The little General actually saluted the younger officer, while in the muddy, rain-sodden fields and ditches his men whispered, 'Did you see who his nibs was. Christ, *him* right up there! Wonders will never cease . . .'

A little later, the little General was giving the same sort of pep talk to yet another battalion commander. 'Now this is the way you're going to do it, Colonel. You'll go straight

153

down this road, leapfrogging companies as soon as things get too sticky for an individual company. To your left and right flanks you'll be supported by a brigade of Churchill tanks and, believe you me, another kind of support the like of which you've never seen in your life before.'

'Yessir . . . thank you, sir,' the CO, whose last battle had been Dunkirk four years before, said. 'My chaps will appreciate any kind of help they can get. This is their first time up, sir.'

'I know . . . I know,' the little General said somewhat testily, as if he didn't want to hear that sort of talk. In the ditch to his left, the medics were working on a bunch of casualties. He could hear the moans and sharp commands of the angry doctors, as they worked all out, ripping open uniforms, stemming the flow of blood, injecting, bandaging, painting the morphine dosage on the foreheads of the unconscious men.

As he encouraged the CO, he promised himself he'd give the divisional surgeon a ballocking for this. Men going up for the first time shouldn't be exposed to their own wounded. The poor blighters should have been transported further back to a field dressing station. Aloud he said, 'We've got something special up our sleeve this time. Save lives. We'll knock the Hun for six this time, believe you me, Colonel.'

It was then that the little General heard the first muted roar to the west for which he had been waiting all this time. He broke off in mid-sentence. He cocked his head to one side like a chirpy little bird. There was no mistaking it. It was them. At last. To the front where the lead units of the 59th Division waited at their start line, the signal flares started to hiss into the dark wet sky. It was a signal to the newcomers where the British front ended and the enemy one commenced.

The little General had no more time for the infantry. He signalled for his Humber staff car, hardly bothering to salute the young CO. Hurriedly his aides tossed the rest of the Woodbines to the troops, their faces turned upwards in the rain, listening to that strange sound, too, wondering what it could be.

The little General knew what it was. It gave him pleasure. At last he was going to take Caen. Ever since he had realized that Caen was going to be a tougher nut than he'd thought and the Yanks had begun complaining about the slowness – 'Why, those limeys spend half their time sitting on their keisters drinking tea' – he had pleaded with Air to give him the support of a massive air attack. Bomber Harris and his 'Brylcreem boys' had been obstinate. They thought they'd win the war by bombing Germany's factories. Soldiers weren't needed, except to occupy ground; the bombers would suffice. Sometimes he had wondered angrily whether the damned Air Ministry was actually part of the British Armed Forces and on his side. In the end Churchill himself had intervened. He had made a special appeal to 'Bomber Harris' and the stone-faced air marshal, who boasted he killed thousands of Germans every day, had given in; after all Churchill could be a very awkward man if he chose to be.

Now as General Bernard Law Montgomery, the 'little General', finally allowed one of his aides to slip a 'Briths warm' over his soaked battledress, he sat back in the big staff car, confident that within the next twenty-four hours, Caen would be his at last and the Battle for Normandy would be over.

Two

The whole of Caen quaked and trembled under the tremendous bombardment. From end to end of the horizon red lights blinked like the open mouths of enormous blast furnaces. The din was awesome. It battered the men's ears almost physically. Time and time again as shells started from the gigantic naval guns off the coast, they opened their mouths like automatons to prevent their eardrums from being shattered. As for the land-based artillery barrage, the shells came in a constant stream, filling the acrid-stinking air in one continuous scream of fury, broken only by the sharp, piercing crack as they burst.

Now to the front of von Dodenburg's positions, the Caen suburb was nothing more than a collection of smoking ruins: heaps of broken masonry, from which charred timbers and grotesquely twisted girders protruded, still glowing a dull purple from the fires. Here and there a gas main exploded and added its fire and flames to that scene of death and destruction.

The survivors cowered in their pits. They hugged the earth like a fervent lover. Unknown to them, they screamed and shrieked like crazy men. Soaked as they were with the pelting rain, they soiled themselves anew with their own waste. They trembled and shook with every fresh boom of an exploding shell. Gasping and choking in the acrid fumes, they covered their wild, staring eyes with trembling hands like little children trying to blot out some unpleasant dream.

And all the while, it rained and rained unrelentingly.

The raindrops lashed the churned-up earth, slashing the men's skinny backs, swamping their little holes. It was as if some God on high had sickened of the human race and was determined to wash these miserable creatures from the face of his earth for good.

But now new horror presented itself. For a while the thunder of the artillery and the roar of that grey storm had blotted out the other sound coming from the west. But now there was no mistaking the roar of five hundred of Bomber Harris's four-engined Halifax and Lancaster bombers. Already signal flares were floating through the rain-heavy sky to mark out their positions.

The German flak, what was left of it, took up the challenge. Shells started to explode about the lead flight. The four-engine bombers didn't seem to notice. They came on in a dead-straight line, heading for the centre of the French city. An aircraft disappeared in a bright, white flash. One minute it was there; the next it had vanished completely. Another was hit and started to limp to the ground, trailing black smoke behind it. A third had its port wing shot off. The wing fluttered down like a great metallic leaf. Still the others came on, as if nothing would stop them now. They were Bomber Harris's boys; nothing ever stopped them reaching their targets.

Below, the defenders of the Hitlerjugend dared not even look upwards. They huddled ever deeper in their holes, as the terrific artillery bombardment stopped with startling suddenness, leaving a loud, echoing silence behind it. Von Dodenburg knew what that meant. The ground assault force was already leaving the start line; the artillery didn't want to kill their own infantry. As soon as the bombers were finished with their work of sudden death and destruction, the infantry would attack. He raised his voice to warn the men, but found he couldn't speak. The next moment there was the whistle of the first sticks of bombs coming hurtling down. The destruction of Caen had commenced.

In the basement of the great Convent of St-Saveur, only

half a kilometre from where Kuno von Dodenburg prepared for the last battle, Nurse Bogex, who had once tended him, supported herself against the ancient wall of the basement and stared around at the ashen, frightened faces of her charges. Brave and practical as always, she knew she must do something. If she didn't, there'd be a panic. Even the Huns seemed to have given up. She opened her mouth, wet her lips and began with 'Ave Maria' . . .

Now the aerial bombardment had reached its climax. The air crews, their bombs gone, were attempting to joke about their profession with: 'Now we've finished working for the government. Now we're working for ourselves. Let's get the hell out of here.' Squadron by squadron, they turned, a bomber here and there trailing smoke from a damaged engine, and started to head for home, and bacon and eggs. And down below, among the throng of frightened people packed into the great Cathedral of St-Etienne, in which lay the body of William the Conqueror, who had invaded England nearly a thousand years before, an angry priest shook his fist from the pulpit and cried, 'Perish the day, my friends, that Duke William ever conquered perfidious England!'

'If only the rain would stop,' one of the 'Baby Division' survivors cried. In another pit a grenadier, his legs blown off, dragged himself over the rim and tried to crawl to where von Dodenburg crouched. 'For God's sake, sir, use your pistol on me. I'm a cripple, no more a man. Please . . . pistol.' His desperate plea was cut short by the death rattle. His face dropped forward into the mud and was silent. Relentlessly the raindrops continued to beat on his head.

Matz wiped away the black hair-dye that trickled down the side of his wizened face in the rain and with blood-scummed, quivering lips, croaked, 'You've got to do something, sir . . .' He swallowed hard, holding his head to one side, as if he could only get breath that way. 'You've got to make a decision, sir.'

'*Halt die Schnauze*, lowlife,' Schulze cried. 'Hold your

158

trap. Can't you see the CO's got enough on his plate as it is!'

Von Dodenburg was listening to Schulze, the only one who seemed in control of his emotions after that tremendous pounding. 'What decision?' he asked, his voice seeming to come from a long way away, so that he could hardly recognize it as his own.

'Surrender, sir, or make a run for it.'

Von Dodenburg looked at the corporal in horror. 'You can't mean that, Matz,' he gasped. 'I can't surrender . . . I can't run for it. Nor can you. You're Wotan—'

'Of course, the Bavarian barnshitter doesn't mean it, sir,' Schulze chimed in hastily. 'All them Bavarians are a bit weak in the head. Lots of incest in Bavaria, everybody knows that.'

Doggedly Matz said, ignoring the insult to his native country, 'If we don't do something soon, sir, there'll be none of us left. Look over there, sir. Old Flipper, dead as a duck, and these lads –' he indicated the ashen trembling teenage grenadiers – 'They've shat their pants long ago. What are their mothers gonna say, sir. I wouldn't like to have them on *my* conscience.'

Schulze acted. He grabbed Matz's collar with his hamlike fist and hauled him right off his feet, so that Matz's wooden leg creaked alarmingly. 'Watch your lip, plush ears! One more word out of you, Matz, and I'll stick yer wooden leg so far up yer dirty arse that yer glassy orbs will pop out of their sockets! Now no more talk like that to the CO. He's got enough—'

'All right, all right,' von Dodenburg attempted to pacify the big Hamburger, his face red with fury at what he regarded as the betrayal of his friendship by his old running mate Matz. 'I understand. I understand only too well. Let me promise you this. When they come –' he meant the assault infantry, for already he could hear the rumble of the enemy tanks further down the shattered streets and the hoarse cries of the advancing infantry of the 'Staffs' – 'we'll give 'em a bloody nose. I think we ought to do that and then we retreat. What do you say to that, comrades?'

For a moment they hesitated, while Matz hung his head, as if he were suddenly ashamed of himself. But Schulze wouldn't let his CO be affronted by a refusal. He raised his voice against the sudden angry snap and crackle of the new small-arms battle: 'What's wrong with you dogs? Do you want to live for ever? Of course we'll fight on. We're the SS . . . More, we're frigging Assault Regiment Wotan!'

The appeal did the trick. Suddenly they were yelling their heads off, pale faces abruptly animated by new enthusiasm. Even Matz was caught up with it. He cried: *'Heil Wotan . . . !'*

The English came as they always did, bravely but stupidly, or so a tense von Dodenburg told himself. They never used the cover of tanks to shield their infantry as German tactics did. Instead of using the 'grape',* they came in open formation, which made ideal targets for both snipers and short-range mortar crews.

Now the enemy bombardment, aerial and artillery, had ceased totally. Unlike a German attack when both infantry and armour would use 'marching fire', the Tommies advanced without fire support. It was good they did so. The defenders were slowly coming to, aware of the rain once more, as it continued to beat down, chilling them to the bone and making them aware of where they were and what was happening. Here and there they started to poke their heads up higher above their parapets, bringing their weapons to bear while the mortar crews, what were left of them, prepared to bring their tubes into action.

'Hold your fire, men,' von Dodenburg ordered softly. 'Pass it on.'

*Soldiers pressed tightly together behind the tank protection. *'Traube'* in German. *Transl.*

The order went from man to man, as the enemy infantry came ever closer, the lone Churchill tank clambering and slithering over the piles of smoking rubble, its stubby cannon searching from left to right for an enemy who seemed to have vanished. Now despite the pouring rain, von Dodenburg could make out the officers, his men's first targets. They were easy to identify. Their binoculars slung round their young necks, their map cases and revolvers instead of the ordinary soldier's rifle, gave them away at once. Von Dodenburg shook his head at such stupidity. How green could combat soldiers get? He concluded that this must be a new division that the Englishman Montgomery had thrown into the line in a desperate attempt to capture Caen at last.

Then he forgot the English greenhorns and concentrated on those under his command. 'Schulze,' he said softly, as if the advancing Tommies might well hear him, 'officers and NCOs first.'

'*Jawohl*,' Schulze agreed with some of his old relish, raising his machine pistol and aiming it at a fat sergeant whose white stripes of rank were clearly visible. 'Porky will do for starters.' With a little grunt, he pressed his trigger. The weapon slammed against his big shoulder, spitting fire. The fat sergeant flung up his arms, his stomach ripped apart in an instant, his intestines, grey and steaming, sliding out of him like some marker rope.

That first burst seemed to act as a signal.

Now the defenders opened up on all sides. The attackers went down, whirling round, arms waving in a frenzy, dancing, it seemed, to some crazy tune at the command of a mad puppet-master. It wasn't a battle; it was a massacre. Desperately the officers and NCOs still on their feet tried to rally their surviving men. For a few moments it appeared they might do so. The South Staffs might be green, but they were brave. But then some bold 'baby' of the Hitlerjugend strode right into the middle of the road, directly in the path of the nearest lumbering Churchill. He paused there, ignoring

161

the bullets cutting the air all about him, legs spread like some Western gunslinger in a Hollywood film, rocket launcher poised on his shoulder, taking aim calmly.

'Get yer stupid skinny arse out of the way,' Schulze yelled frantically, 'or yer'll get it shot off!'

The boy ignored the warning. In the very same instant that the Churchill's machine gun ripped his skinny chest apart, he fired his missile. It slammed into the tank. A purple glow. The smell and stink of metal melting. The tank shuddered. It came to an abrupt stop. Next moment it exploded in a sheet of violent flame. It was then that the surviving South Staffs turned and ran.

'Cease fire . . . Cease fire, will you,' von Dodenburg called almost angrily as the 'babies' continued to fire at the fleeing Tommies. 'Don't waste your ammo . . .'

The words died on his lips, as Matz called across to him, his face blackened with explosives, his blouse in tatters, 'There's a funny sound coming this way, sir.'

'What?'

'A funny sound over there.' He pointed a dirty, bloody hand to the left of the wrecked Churchill, a charred crew member half-hanging out of the turret, tiny greedy blue flames licking at his dead body. 'Can't make it out, sir.'

'Like the trams back in Hamburg before the war, sir,' Schulze tried to help.

Von Dodenburg raised his head cautiously higher and above the protection of the brick rubble. Despite the drumbeat of the new barrage and steady hiss of the rainstorm, he could hear it, too, now.

Schulze was right: it was like the whirr of the electric trams back home. Still very cautious in case the Tommies had left a concealed sniper behind, he searched that lunar landscape for the cause of the strange sound. But for a few moments he could see nothing but the wreckage, the smashed Churchill and the dead bodies of the Tommies. Then he spotted it.

Emerging from the drifting smoke came a small squat

162

slug-like object crawling forward and towards them at a snail's pace. There was something eerie and a little frightening about the purposefulness of the strange device and the weird whirring noise it gave off. Then von Dodenburg remembered. Back at Anzio they had used similar devices against the newly landed Tommies. 'It's one of our Goliaths,' he yelled in sudden alarm, 'and it's packed with two hundred pounds of high explosive!'

Three

Earlier that year when Wotan had been rushed to the Anzio beachhead in Italy in an attempt to stop the Anglo-Americans from breaking out from the coast and driving for Rome, von Dodenburg had watched two Goliaths, worked by engineers, being employed against a British infantry company.

At first he had taken the two devices, mini-tanks being operated by electric cables, for something akin to kids' toys. As Schulze had commented as they lay in the sand dunes watching the snail-like progress of the new secret weapon, 'I hope they're having fun, sir. Sooner or later them engineers'll have to piss or get off the pot. And then it'll be Wotan's turn. We'll have to do the hammering.'

But Schulze had been mistaken. The first one had struck a bunker, which they were told later had held half a company of British infantry. When they'd gone down to inspect the damage, they'd found severed heads and limbs everywhere, the sand red with the blood of the dead. Not a single Tommy had survived the devastating explosion.

Now the English must have found a supply of the frightening devices and were employing them against their inventors. Suddenly von Dodenburg woke up to the danger of their position here in the rubble. If he didn't act soon, they might very well end up like that savaged British infantry company. He had to do something – anything – and he had to do it soon. Otherwise . . .

He didn't think that terrifying thought to an end. Abruptly

164

he was on his feet, desperation pumping adrenalin through his weary body, charging it with new energy. Suddenly he was up and running, springing over piles of rubble, ignoring single shots from hidden English infantry. 'Sir,' Schulze yelled after him. 'For God's sake, sir . . .' His words trailed away to nothing. Von Dodenburg, running all out, his arms working like pistons, wasn't listening. That was clear to the big NCO.

Von Dodenburg's mind was elsewhere. Already his ears had taken in the faint electric whirr of another of the frightening devices close by. The Tommies were going to blast them out of their positions. They'd show no mercy now. Von Dodenburg ran on, going all out, realizing as he ran that this was the end of the road, one way or another. It was up to him. No one else could save his kids, but him.

And there it was: coming straight at him, heading for the 'babies'' positions with grim inexorability. Behind it, slithering through the rubble, were the two electric cables being controlled by some unseen Tommy. He paused and crouched, sobbing for breath, fighting to control his breathing. He knew what to do. But would the Tommies, wherever they were hiding, let him? Naturally the operator would be supported by riflemen. Perhaps they had spotted him already. But once he made a move towards the Goliath they would react; there was no denying that.

Sergeant Schulze knew that, too. Standing upright, throwing caution to the winds, he yelled above the drumbeat of the pouring rain, 'All right, you lunch of piss-pansies. Don't just sit there, yer frigging thumbs up yer frigging arses – give the CO covering fire.'

That roused them. Now they opened wild, unaimed fire on the rubble behind the advancing mini-tank, knowing the enemy would be there somewhere, while von Dodenburg tensed and readied himself for what he had to do: grab the electric cables and pull them for all he was worth, hoping that he would succeed and stop the devilish contraption from moving. He took a deep breath and counted to three. Next moment he dived and grabbed the cables, feeling the strain in his shoulders almost at once. It was as if someone had just thrust a red-hot poker into his shoulder muscles. Desperately he hung on as the Goliath pulled him through the rubble, the sharp bricks ripping and tearing at his body mercilessly. Still he hung on, knowing he had only seconds left.

'Come on, you bastards,' he cursed through gritted teeth. 'Give, won't you? For God's sake – *give!*'

Now the Goliath was only a matter of twenty metres from the Wotan positions. Already the young soldiers were beginning to cease firing and duck back into the holes, knowing what was going to come. 'Keep firing . . . *Um Himmelswillen – weitermachen*,' Schulze cried, as Matz lobbed his last stick grenade at the area where they thought the English controlling the devilish device might be hiding. '*LOS!*'

The exploding grenade had no effect. Now the English were firing at von Dodenburg. He tugged and ripped at the obstinate cables as the bullets whipped up the mud all around. Still the silent monster, packed with enough explosive to kill most of the defenders, kept on moving. Von Dodenburg, his muscles afire, bit his bottom lip till the blood came, willing the cables to break, trying to ignore the agony of his burning palms. A few metres away, Schulze cried, 'Let go, sir . . . It's no use . . . Let's go while there's still time.'

If von Dodenburg heard the shout, he ignored it. He gave one last mighty tug. The soft whirring stopped. The Goliath ground to a halt. Von Dodenburg fell face forward into the mud, sobbing for breath in the same instant that the bullet slammed into the side of his helmet, penetrated it and whacked into his skull, and everything want black. An instant later, unconscious, he was unaware of a handful of his men picking him up out of the mud and bearing him away, while the rest fled, throwing away their weapons in panic as they went, the role of the 'Baby Division' in the Battle of Normandy over at last . . .

*   *   *

166

As he did every day, Field Marshal Rommel visited the front. A little later, almost to the minute when von Dodenburg suffered his wound, he went to the headquarters of SS General Dietrich, his fellow conspirator in the plan to kill Hitler. For Dietrich, that time could not come quickly enough. As he told the Field Marshal, his breath smelling strongly of the cognac he had been drinking solidly all day, 'My SS divisions are being bled white, Marshal. This cannot go on. We of the SS have done more than enough for the Führer in this war. Time must have a stop.'

Rommel did not comment on the fighting ability of the SS. He knew they had achieved major victories in the past, but the cost had been high in manpower and materiel; SS commanders were always very wasteful of their men. Instead he said, 'You need not wait much longer, Dietrich. He won't listen to reason. Therefore he must die.' Even now with only hours to go before Hitler was to be assassinated, these powerful men, with thousands and hundreds of thousands of men under their command, dared not mention the intended victim by name.

At four, Rommel set off in his car for his HQ. He was anxious to get back to Army Group because he had just heard of the breakthrough on the Hitlerjugend front. But it wasn't going to be that easy. Up ahead his driver could see that the damned Allied *Jabos* had been working over German transport. Trucks and lighter vehicles littered the road, shot up and in flames. Reluctantly, knowing that it would entail serious delays, he turned the big car off on to secondary and – hopefully – safer roads. But that wasn't to be.

They were just outside the small French town of Vimoutiers when the sergeant bodyguard shouted urgently, '*Tiefflieger* . . . *Achtung* . . . enemy dive bomber!'

The driver, Private Daniel, knew what to do; after all he was the Army Group Commander's driver and proud of the honour. He put his foot down hard on the gas. If he could reach the side road to the right some two hundred metres away, he knew he could find cover. The big tourer shot forward.

But the British pilot wasn't going to be shaken off that easily. He came barrelling in at 400 miles an hour, cannon blazing, pumping tracer shells at the fleeing car. Rommel threw his head back to look. In that same moment a salvo of shells ripped the length of the car. He yelled with sudden pain as something hot, burning, searing penetrated his left temple. In front of him, Daniel, the driver, hit in the left shoulder and arm, tried frantically to maintain control of the car. In vain. As Rommel slumped forward, already unconscious, the driver let go of the steering wheel. The next moment, the car hit a tree stump, skidded across the road and overturned in the right-hand ditch.

Rommel flew out of the wrecked car and lay unconscious in the middle of the road as the second British aircraft zoomed in, firing its cannon, and attempted to drop bombs on those lying on the road. In frustration and anger, Rommel's aide drew his pistol and loosed off wild shots as the plane flew directly over the prostrate Field Marshal, dragging its evil black shadow behind, its prop wash whipping the foliage into a wild dance.

As useless as the shots were, they seemed to do the trick. For the attacker veered away and didn't come in for a second run. A few moments later both planes were streaking back westwards to their forward airfields, pleased probably with this day's work, leaving a dying Rommel behind. The day before, Rommel had forwarded a top-secret report to Hitler, stating that: 'Our troops are fighting heroically but even so the end of this unequal battle is in sight.' In his own hand, the Field Marshal had added a postscript. It read: 'I must beg you to recognize at once the political significance of this situation. I feel it is my duty, as the Commander in Chief of the Army Group, to say this plainly.' As he had sealed the letter he had cried aloud, as if appealing to some God on high, 'Make peace, you fool . . . make peace!'

But it was too late for that now. No one could – or would – replace the one-time 'Desert Fox'. The central figure of the generals' plot to dispose of Hitler and make a separate peace in the West had been eliminated, not by the Gestapo, but by two cocky teenage pilots. Now both Britain, the victor, and Germany, the vanquished, would be ruined by the war and the USA was on its way to becoming the world's 'super-duper' power . . .

Four

N ow while Field Marshal Rommel fought his last battle
with death, Kuno von Dodenburg remained unconscious, unaware of the fact that the world was beginning to
change drastically around him. Schulze and Matz had taken
charge, shooing away most of the young 'baby' soldiers
like an adult might chase away a group of importuning
schoolkids. 'Go home . . . go home to mother, you silly
shits . . . She might comfort yer with a bit o' titty!' Matz
had cried, his face red with fury, the raindrops shaken from
the rim of his battered helmet. 'The war's over, you bunch of
cardboard soldiers. Over . . . don't you frigging understand
that? OVER!'

The survivors had stared at him open-mouthed, as if
they couldn't understand the world, as Schulze cradled the
unconscious CO in his brawny arms like a baby and carried
him to the sole surviving half-track. Moments later as Matz
started to drive away, followed by a salvo of mortar-bombs,
the 'babies' of the shattered Hitler Youth Division were still
standing there in complete bewilderment, rooted to the spot
as if for ever.

It was Matz who made the real, decisive decision, however.
'Schulzi,' he called over his shoulder, as Schulze applied a
shell dressing to the CO's wounded head, 'we're not stopping
here. If we do, the 'chained dogs' will nab us and in zero,
comma, nothing we'll be in some alarm company getting our
arses shot off agen.'

'But what about the CO? He needs attention urgently.

170

That means we've got to get him to a field dressing station.'

'I know . . . I know,' Matz shouted narrowly, missing a great smoking crater in the middle of the road. 'You're forgetting the Frog hospital . . . at St-Saveur. We'll find one of those Frog doctors who can patch him up till we can get back to the Reich to a better hospital.'

Schulze digested the information for a minute or two, as another artillery bombardment crashed into the dying Norman city. '*Einverstanden* – agreed, Matz. But it's going to be shitting risky.'

'Even breathing these days is shitting risky,' Matz commented bitterly, as if suddenly he had a grudge against the whole world. 'Come on, let's get on with it.'

That had been the start of their odyssey, though the two old running mates didn't know it at the time, for on that day everything was in a state of flux with even an SS general, 'Panzermeyer', the new commander of what was left of the Hitlerjugend, defying a 'Führer Order' and commanding the survivors to abandon Caen and take up new positions to the east of the dying city. 'We were meant to die in Caen,' he told his staff, leaning on the rifle he habitually carried just like his ordinary soldiers, 'but I'll be damned if I'm going to sacrifice my boys to a senseless order.'

Thus it was that when the battered half-track pulled up outside the great Convent of St-Saveur and Schulze and Matz started looking for a doctor to attend to their wounded CO, the German presence had vanished and already armed youths of the French Resistance were coming out of their hiding places seeking revenge for what had happened this July to their native city.

St-Saveur was in a state of absolute chaos. The time for prayer was over. Now it was everyone for himself. There were panic-stricken refugees from the city outside, fighting to get into the convent, and those inside, fearful that the great convent would be just another target for the

Anglo-Americans, fighting to get out while there was still time. There were crazy nuns attempting to pull off their habits and expose their deathly white bodies to any man wishing to see it, as if they had wasted a lifetime with chastity and wanted to enjoy the pleasures of the flesh before it was too late. There were equally mad old men, also naked, fondling their flaccid penises which had not savoured sexual excitement these many years, urging themselves to have an erection. Self-important officials in white overalls but wearing military-style *kepis* and jackboots strode back and forth, noting God knows what on their clipboards, shouting silly orders over their shoulders at weeping secretaries, as if they were still in charge of things.

But to Schulze and Matz it seemed that no one was still in charge in this crazy world of underground chambers which stank of ether, sweat and human misery. Even the presence of the two battle-dirty SS men carrying machine pistols and carrying a wounded officer excited no interest. The French were too concerned with their own fate. Thus it was that the three of them fought their way through the crowded rooms looking for help like ghosts, totally unnoticed, the sight of those silver SS runes and skull-and-crossbones badges no longer causing that spine-chilling fear that they had once.

But when the two NCOs were just about to give up ever finding medical assistance, a voice in accented German called, 'Colonel von Dodenburg and you, Sergeant . . . Sergeant . . .'

They lowered their burden and turned as one, and there she was – Nurse Bogex, her pretty face white with shock, as she pushed and thrust her way through the panicked throng to reach them. Schulze gave a gasp of relief. 'Matzi, old house,' he breathed, 'I think we've struck lucky at last.'

But Matz was too worn and at the same time relieved to do anything but nod his head, the dye from his rain-soaked head still dripping down his face.

The next three or four hours passed in nerve-racking hectic

activity. Nurse Bogex had conquered her tears at the sight of the badly wounded Kuno almost at once. Swiftly, with the aid of the two SS men, she brought a series of doctors to see the wounded man. Some came willingly making no distinction between a wounded Frenchman and a wounded German; they were both God's children, human beings.

Others were reluctant, prepared to refuse seeing the '*sale Boche*' until Schulze or Matz intervened with '*nix sale Boche*', jamming the muzzles of their machine pistols into the reluctant doctors' ribs to convince them, which they naturally did, that a good doctor was dedicated to the service of humanity.

But at the end of the series of forced, hurried examinations, the doctors' findings were not very encouraging. Nurse Bogex translated the diagnosis of the professor who saw the unconscious man as that terrible day drew to a close: 'He says that Kuno – your colonel – will pull through and, in due course, perhaps even by tomorrow he will regain consciousness.' She paused and her face grew even graver as she translated the bearded little professor's final assessment. 'However, there is a danger that Kuno might have lost his sight.'

Even the virtually unshockable Sergeant Schulze was thunderstruck. 'Miss, that can't be possible,' he blurted out, red face suddenly drained of colour. 'The CO . . . well, he's the CO. He can't be blind.'

The little French professor seemed to understand, for he nodded his head, face grave, and said, '*Oui, c'est vrai!*' Then he rose and was gone, leaving the three of them – the French nurse and the two old hares – staring down at the unconscious figure of von Dodenburg, frozen into a shocked tableau of horror and compassion.

But in the course of that night when the young men of the city went on a wild rampage, looting the stores the Germans had left behind, seizing weapons from the German arsenals, shooting lone Germans who had been left behind or had gone into hiding, waiting to surrender to the British and Canadians, who were now entering Caen, Nurse Bogex took the two old hares into a secluded corner of the great grey convent's cellars and by the flickering light of a stump of a candle, drew a rough sketch map of the city area in the age-old dust of the place.

'Your division, what's left of it, has retreated to here,' she explained, the sound of wild firing penetrating even through the thick walls of the cellars, 'to the Carpigny Airfield area. Between them and your 21st Panzer Division, there is a gap which hasn't been penetrated by the English.' For a moment she paused and ran her hand lovingly across an unconscious von Dodenburg's forehead.

It was that gesture that convinced Schulze he could trust her implicitly, though he knew he had to ask the question which had been troubling him for hours now. 'How do you know such things – you a civvy nurse?'

She hesitated only an instant for she knew she could trust these rough-looking SS NCOs, too. They could have saved themselves by abandoning their blinded CO. But they hadn't; that was enough for her. 'Because I belong to the Resistance. I have for a long time. I was sent to spy on you *Bo*— Germans. I know such things. Now I want to use them to our advantage.'

'To our advantage?' Matz queried.

'Yes. I shall not leave Kuno here,' she declared stoutly. 'He will get no treatment. And the way the young men outside are behaving, he will not survive if they get their dirty paws on him. They will show no mercy. So . . .' She shrugged in the Gallic fashion, her delightful little breasts rising, the nipples hard, as if she were suddenly very cold beneath her thin white smock. 'So we must escape.'

'Escape – to where?' Schulze asked.

'I don't know exactly. But definitely out of this mad place. Here we – you don't stand a chance. We must go east through the gap I mentioned. Then we shall see.' She said the words like some determined matriarch, dealing with her slightly stupid offspring. 'Clear?'

'Clear,' the two running mates replied at once.

'So this is what we must do. I have a *gazogène* –' she meant a gas-powered vehicle – 'hidden behind the hospital. We of the Resistance used it occasionally. The bag is full of gas – it will last till we find something better. What I need now is medical supplies, some food, water—'

'Water,' Schulze began contemptuously, 'never drink water; dogs piss in it.' Then he changed his mind and became serious again. 'Go on, miss. What else?'

'Something to bribe with,' she continued. 'Cigarettes, drink, anything that will oil the long road ahead. I know my fellow countrymen, Sergeant Schulze. These last years of defeat and occupation have corrupted France. They need to be bribed.'

Matz slapped the butt of his machine pistol. 'And if bribes don't work, M'selle Bogex, this little pea-shooter will. Come on, Schulze, what are you sitting there for like a spare penis at a wedding. Finger out of the orifice, let's see what we can find in the way of bribes.' He rose and looked at the nurse and von Dodenburg. 'Will you be all right, miss, while we're away?'

She forced a smile and lifted her smock slightly. Tied to her belt underneath there was a small ivory-handled lady's pistol. 'I'll be all right,' she answered. 'It won't be the first time I've used this.' She covered it up hastily. 'Now then, off you go. *Bonne chance.*'

Two hours later, they were on the way in the ancient Citroën, with the great gas bag flapping and billowing on the roof, through the burning streets of the old city, its gutters littered with dead and drunken young Frenchmen, who were firing wildly into the bright-red sky, and with Schulze uttering his usual cry on occasions like this when things were desperate – and there had been many of them in these past terrible years: 'BUY COMBS, LADS . . . THERE'S LOUSY TIMES AHEAD . . .'

Five

Very slowly, Matz drove the old car down the country road. There was abandoned and shot-up equipment everywhere, resembling the aftermath of a terrible flood. Everywhere there were broken-down, abandoned vehicles, dead transport horses with swollen bellies and legs sticking up stiffly, so that they looked like tethered barrage balloons. And the dead.

The corpses of those done to death from the sky by the merciless Allied fighter-bombers were on all sides, an untidy carpet of field grey lining the ditches and the fields to either side of the country road. Already the crows and other carrion had descended upon the bodies picking at the eyes, noses, ears, and other soft and tender parts of the slain soldiers, bickering and squabbling with each other when they found a particularly tasty titbit. Even the traffic passing by in a solid stream didn't deter them. They simply flapped their wings sullenly, but went on feasting.

In the centre of the road, the peasants and the occasional military crawled on, with no eyes for the dead. Their gaze was set firmly on the horizon to the east, away from this savage slaughter. To Schulze sitting next to Matz in the Citroën, machine pistol lying on his lap ready for instant action, it appeared that all the barns, garages, farms of Western France had opened their doors to discharge this mass of vehicles. There were clumsy bullock-drawn farm carts, ancient aristocratic carriages drawn by emaciated thoroughbreds, wood-burning, rickety pre-war cars, their boilers puffing and steaming behind them, looking as if they might explode at any moment; long wickerwork baskets on wheels used to transport the crippled, even wheelbarrows in which were perched ancient grannies with shawls thrown over their silver heads. Anything with wheels had been pressed into service to carry these frightened men, women and children, civilians and soldiers away from the disaster soon to come.

But Schulze, the veteran, knew that it was not only there where disaster lurked; they might well encounter it in front of them too. What if they met a German stop line, manned by the 'chained dogs' or even their own SS comrades; they'd show no mercy with anyone in uniform who they thought was trying to use this civilian convoy to desert. It would be a five-minute, three-officer 'flying tribunal'; two minutes more and the guilty party would be dangling from a rope on the nearest tree. He sniffed and wished he could belt a stiff drink behind his collar, telling himself he couldn't relax for a moment; all their fates depended upon his cunning and swift reaction.

He turned and looked at the back where Nurse Bogex cradled von Dodenburg's bandaged head in her lap. The CO's eyes were still closed and he was breathing heavily, but in the last few hours since they had set off from a dying Caen, von Dodenburg had groaned a couple of times. The Frenchwoman had assured Schulze that the CO was in no real pain. The groans had been occasioned by the movement of the ancient Citroën. They meant his level of unconsciousness had become shallower. He'd probably regain consciousness fairly soon. It was something that Schulze prayed would happen; then they could assess if the CO was really blinded. Now he mouthed the question: 'Any signs?'

She shook her head and said, 'No.'

Schulze gave a faint smile and, turning his head, resumed his watch, as next to him, Matz throttled back yet again. The traffic was beginning to slow down once more and by craning his neck, Schulze could see why. There was a narrow bridge ahead, slowing down the refugees into a single column. He nudged Matz. 'Keep yer eyes peeled,' he ordered.

'Like a tin of tomatoes.' Matz gave the traditional reply. 'Going for a look-see?'

'Yes,' Schulze answered, slinging his machine pistol over his head and slipping a stick grenade into the side of his right back boot.

'Watch yer back.'

'I will, don't you worry yer pretty little head.' With that, he started towards the head of the column, unregarded by the mixed bunch of civilians and soldiers, whose gaze was fixed on the other side of the river, as if it were the Promised Land itself.

Cautiously he approached the bridge. What was causing the hold-up, he wasn't sure, but he could guess. Either the engineers were busy preparing to blow the structure up or there was a 'chained dog' stop line on the other side. Whatever the cause was, it was, Schulze told himself grimly, a problem; and at this stage of the game, Schulze was not prepared to tolerate problems. He gripped his machine pistol more tightly in his big, hard paws and knew that if it came down to it, the gun in his hands would solve most problems.

Surprisingly enough, however, Schulze wouldn't have to resort to what he called his 'pea-shooter' this particular July day. For as he reached a large camouflaged truck, red cross emblems painted all over it, including the roof, indicating that someone was trying to escape the debacle by posing as German Medical Corps troops, a familiar trick in retreats, his ears were assailed by a voice singing drunkenly in a thick East Westphalian accent. It seemed somehow familiar, as did the smell of frying sausage coming from the back of the large truck.

For a moment, the problems of the bridge and what lay ahead were forgotten. His nostrils twitched from side to side and slowly the saliva began to trickle down the sides of his unshaven chin. He licked his lips hungrily. '*Bratwurst!*' he muttered to himself. 'Noble German fried sausage. Worth giving yer left ball for.' He approached the back of the truck and heard the slap of a hand on what he took to be a bare female rump, followed by a shrieked, 'Why, I didn't think generals did that sort of thing, Kurt.'

'You'd be surprised what generals do – or in my case, did, my little cabbage,' a hoarse old man's voice croaked. 'My God, woman, you've got a better rump on you than most nags I've ever ridden in my long life.'

'You naughty boy,' a female voice that seemed somehow familiar, though Schulze couldn't quite place it, replied. 'You carry on like that, General, and I shall have to punish you – *severely*! You understand?'

'I understand. Punish, eh? With a horsewhip? Remember how old I am, my sweet little cabbage. Perhaps a switch might be less severe for my age?' the man quavered. '*What?*'

'We shall see. Now then, let me finish my sausage . . . Keep your filthy hands to yourself. You don't know where they've been.'

Schulze, anxious yet curious to know where those 'filthy hands' were, though he could hazard a guess, forgot that particular problem for a moment, as hoarse shouts at the bridge indicated that something was going on there now. He pushed by the large camouflaged truck until he came parallel with the driver, who said with a note of relief when he saw the big noncom, 'Thank God the SS has arrived, *Obersturmbannführer*. Those silly bastards are going to blow up the bridge before we cross. I mean they can do what they like to the Frogs, but I've got a general on board back there. Poor imitation of a general officer that he is, he still is a general. They can't do something like that to him.'

'Well, they shitting well seem to be doing it, *Kumpel*,' Schulze growled, as under the direction of a young bespectacled engineer officer, the sappers started to attach sticks of high explosive to each of the bridge's spars, while others in rope slings swung themselves beneath to fix other sticks to the spans. He looked up at the frightened driver. 'All right, start her up and leave this to me.' Cupping his hands around his mouth, he shouted back to Matz, 'Matzi, get ready to move the CO up here – right smartish.' And with that, the big NCO started to push his way through the crowd of gawping French civilians to where the young officer was giving out his orders.

Schulze recognized the type immediately. The officer looked the typical 'rear-echelon stallion', one of those who had spent the war in some staff job at base. His uniform was devoid of decoration save the 'Sports Medal Second Class', and it was still immaculate as if he had come from superior headquarters, where they still thought such things were important. Now he had been turfed out of his nice cushy job and sent to the front where he thought he could play the same old 'rear-echelon stallion' games. Not with Mrs Schulze's handsome son, you can't, Schulze told himself and then, stamping to attention in front of the young officer, he yelled as if he were still back on the parade ground at the SS training school in Bad Tölz, '*Heil Hitler. Oberscharführer Schulze meldet sich zur Stelle!*'

The officer turned, startled, his jaw dropping slightly at the sight of this huge SS NCO, his burly chest covered with decorations, carrying a machine pistol in his hamlike fist as if it was a kid's toy.

He recovered himself and gave a sloppy salute. 'Yes, *Scharführer?*'

'The bridge, sir. Why are you blowing it up, preventing a general officer and a small body of SS Assault Regiment Wotan from carrying out urgent military duties on the other side?' Behind his back, he heard Matz giving orders to Nurse Bogex as they started to carry the CO to the big medical corps truck.

'Why? Because we have been ordered by Army Group HQ to blow up every bridge across the Seine to stop the

damned anglo-Americans.' It was obvious that the young
engineer officer was disconcerted by the sight of this huge
SS NCO who had appeared out of nowhere. All the same,
the man was an NCO and he *was* an officer. 'But what right
have you to question my orders?'

Schulze knew he couldn't waste any more time on the
staff officer. 'This,' he snapped with an unholy grin on his
unshaven dirty face. He slapped the butt of his machine
pistol. Next moment he pressed the trigger. The weapon
burst into angry life. A stream of bullets zipped the length
of the bridge near the officer's polished boots. He jumped
back hurriedly, face suddenly white with fear. Now you can
see who gives the orders here, *Herr Leutnant*,' Schulze said
easily. For good measure he fired another burst over the
heads of the sappers, who were staring at the spectacle in
open-mouthed wonder. Not for long. The burst convinced
them that there was no future in attempting to prepare the
bridge for demolition. They fled, leaving the lone officer to
stare at the big NCO, wondering what had hit him.

He was not the only one. As Schulze hurried back to the
big truck, where Nurse Bogex and Matz were placing the
unconscious von Dodenburg into the stretcher compartment
behind the driver, who was eager to be off, gunning his engine
all the while, Schulze decided it was time to investigate
the smells and sounds coming from the back. Slinging the
machine pistol over his shoulder, he got on to the step and
pulled open the door. What he saw nearly made him drop to
the ground again.

An elderly general officer, dribbling down his white beard
with excitement, was busy polishing the high boots of a
plump woman in a short skirt which revealed she was without
knickers. He was gasping for breath, panting, 'Oh, my little
cabbage, *more . . . more . . . be brutal to me . . . !'*

The plump woman, one hand clasping a large hot sausage,
dripping with fat, the other a switch with which she routinely
slapped the old general's skinny naked rump, growled in

return in between bites, 'I'll be brutal to you, you disgusting old pervert, if you don't keep on polishing. Your arse'll be black and blue for days to come.' She slapped him again and he polished even more vigorously, while she enjoyed the sausage, taking greedy bites of it, the hot fat dripping on to her ample bosom.

For a moment or two the strange spectacle rendered even Schulze speechless, then as the truck lurched forward, the driver hitting the horn hard to get the civilians out of the way, he roared, 'What perverted piggery is this, eh?'

The white-bearded general dropped his cloth, taken completely by surprise, while the plump woman hastily swallowed the rest of her sausage and turning, bellowed back, 'How dare you come barging in on a couple who are betrothed to be married when they are indulging in a little bit of private recreation . . .'

The words died on her greasy lips as the two recognized each other in the very same instant. 'Schulzi,' she cried. '*You!*'

'Lore,' he exclaimed. '*You!*'

It was the Creeper's wife, and his former mistress.

Watching them through the cab's rear window, Matz said to himself a little enviously. 'Holy strawsack, now we've got a frigging honeymoon couple on board as well.' As for the elderly general, he pulled up his trousers to cover his smarting rump and then sadly put the lid on his tin of boot polish. Somehow, he told himself, he wouldn't be needing it for a while now . . .

Six

'*I address you today*,' Hitler said, his voice now lacking the power of the old days, '*and I am doing so for two reasons. First that you shall hear my voice and know that I personally am unhurt and well; and second, so that you shall hear the details about a crime that has no equal in German history.*'

They had parked the big truck at the edge of a large wood, well out of sight of the enemy fighter-bombers prowling the late afternoon sky everywhere looking for targets as the beaten German Army fled eastwards towards Belgium and the Reich beyond. Nurse Bogex was tending von Dodenburg, who still remained unconscious, while Matz and the driver opened cans of 'old man', meat reputedly made from old men from Berlin's workhouses, for the evening meal. The old general with the white beard was fast asleep in the grass, muttering to himself as he slept, while Schulze and Lore had gone deeper into the wood to 'add a little spice to the meal'. To which Matz had grumbled, 'I know what kind of frigging spice you'll be looking for, you lecherous sod.' Schulze had not been offended. He smirked and slipped his big hand around a giggling Lore's ample bottom, saying, 'Rank hath its privileges, Corporal Matz. Play yer cards right and I might let you have seconds one of these days. Now come, beloved, let us gambol through the grass.' She had giggled even more and the general had stirred in his sleep to mutter, 'Give her the whip, man. The mare needs more of the lash.' Whether he was referring to horses or women no one knew or much cared.

Now the ones who had remained behind listened to

the Führer in faraway East Prussia the previous day: '*An extremely small clique of ambitious, unscrupulous and at the same time foolish, criminally stupid officers hatched a plot to remove me and, with me, virtually to exterminate the German High Command. The bomb that was placed by Count von Stauffenberg exploded two metres away from me on my right side. It wounded very seriously a number of my dear collaborators. One of them has died. I personally am entirely unhurt apart from negligible grazes, bruises or burns.*' Matz spat into the wood fire, but said nothing, though his face said everything as Hitler continued. '*That I have been saved is a clear sign of Providence that I am being allowed to live to carry on the great work of our National Socialist cause.*' Then, shouting in that familiar guttural Austrian style of his, he cried, '*We must counter these evil elements at once. If they offer any sign of resistance, WIPE THEM OUT!*'

The radio went dead and Nurse Bogex said, as the old general continued to mumble about ancient lecheries in his sleep, 'Do you want to go back, Corporal?' She indicated the horizon to the east. 'Back to that madhouse. After that.' She indicated the now silent radio.

Matz was not a very intelligent or sensitive man, but he had been at the front long enough to understand. 'What else can we do, M'selle? We're Germans – that explains it all, doesn't it?'

After a moment she nodded. She looked down at von Dodenburg's pale face and stroked his wounded head lovingly. 'I suppose it does. That you're German, yes, that explains it all.' She fell silent and as the light began to fade the three of them stared at the flickering flames of the fire, each wrapped in a brooding cocoon of his own thoughts.

A hundred metres or so away in the heart of the forest, Lore bent low to reveal the full charms of that delightful bottom of hers, saying, 'But Schulzi, my big daddy bear, there are no mushrooms here. All I've found are *Kremplin*.* I don't think it's yet the season for mushrooms, I really don't.'

Lovingly Schulze ran his big paw over her buttocks and squeezed the left one hard. 'I didn't come here to pick mushrooms.' He slipped his hand under her short skirt and felt the smooth silk of her knickers and the pleasant female warmth coming from below the silk. 'If you follow me, cheetah.'

'Oh, you naughty sergeant, you,' she simpered with what she thought was a girlish laugh. 'You're up to your tricks again, aren't you.' His hand wandered under the silk and touched the dampness beneath. 'I don't think you're agen a trick – or two – yourself, beloved, eh?'

'Well, I suppose I'll have to submit to your wickedness. I know you men.' She started to spread her big fleshy legs, as if in anticipation.

At the back of Schulze's bullet head, a cynical little voice commented, 'I'll bet she's had more Westphalian sausage stuck into her than you've had hot dinners, Sergeant Schulze.'

'But the ground'll be hard,' she moaned a little, as he pushed her on her back, though she did keep her legs firmly apart. She was beginning to breathe a little faster too. In a moment, Schulze knew from past experience, she'd be gasping like broken leathern bellows, her eyes screwed firmly closed, crying, 'Don't hurt me . . . Oh, don't hurt me, I'm delicate,' interspersed with harsh demands to 'Stick it in deeper . . . *deeper!*'

But this evening with the rumble of battle a long way off, Schulze was not fated to have his wicked way with naughty Lore from Westphalia; there'd he no 'stick it in deeper', even though Schulze had been planning that little act most of that July day. For suddenly he was startled by a familiar sound: the rusty rattle of steel tracks. He recognized the sound

---

*A type of tasteless German mushroom. *Transl.*

immediately. It was not the soft rubber-tracked noise of the enemy's Sherman tank. These were German tracked vehicles, which meant trouble for them as deserters from the German armed forces.

He grabbed Lore's hand just as she was about to slip down her knickers and hissed, 'Keep yer drawers on.'

'But you were going to be naughty but nice to me,' she protested.

'I'll be very naughty in a minute, if you don't do as I say,' Schulze persisted, as the noise grew ever closer. 'There's trouble brewing. Now keep those drawers of yourn up and let's have a look-see.'

Still protesting, she let herself be led away, as a suddenly worried Schulze unslung his machine pistol, slipped off the safety catch and prepared for the worst . . .

They were two half-tracks, manned by both SS troopers and grim-faced older 'chained dogs', all of them armed to the teeth and very purposeful. Behind them came a Puma armoured car, stubby cannon moving to left and right as they came down the forest road, as if the unseen gunner was expecting trouble at any moment and would welcome blasting all hell out of someone with the turret gun.

It was the kind of heavily armed patrol that could be found everywhere in the rear areas of the broken, retreating German 7th Army, struggling back in confusion from its defeat in France. Its soldiers demoralized and defeated, ready to desert at the drop of a hat, these mixed SS and Military Police patrols were intended to put some stiffener into the backs of the soldiers trying to find their way back to Germany and the presumed safety of the Siegfried Line on the German border with Luxembourg and Belgium, though most of the German High Command thought they would not stop there, if given a choice, but would carry on till they reached their own homes, where they'd go to ground and sit out the rest of the war. These patrols were out to stop that. As their commanders told these mixed SS–'chained dog' commands,

'The motto, comrades, is: "March or croak!" If the front swine won't march, then they croak,' and they'd make their meaning quite clear by slapping their pistol holsters.

Now as the lead half-track swung round the bend in the road, spotted the log fire, the big Medical Corps truck and the men in German uniform sprawled in the grass, seemingly enjoying the last of the sun, the 'chained dogs' thought they had stumbled on yet another bunch of deserting front swine who had to be taught that it was either 'march or croak'. Up in the cab with the SS driver, the senior noncom turned and spoke to the officer in charge, a pasty-faced but ruthless SS captain, who unusually for the elite SS wore an old-fashioned pince-nez. '*Sturmbannführer*, more of them. Shall we stop?'

'*Ja.*' The answer was clear and decisive, although the day had been long and tiring and had included ten firing parties, with twenty reluctant heroes, who had refused to fight any longer for '*Folk, Fatherland und Führer*', being liquidated.

Slowly the first half-track nudged its way over the grassy verge and headed for the campfire, where an alarmed Matz reached for his machine pistol, realizing even as he did so that it was useless offering any kind of resistance; he was too heavily outnumbered and he knew 'chained dogs' of old; they were a bunch of merciless bastards.

Nurse Bogex seemed to think the same. For in the same moment that the leading half-track came to a stop and an SS officer, stepped out, she placed her arms around a still unconscious Kuno von Dodenburg protectively. Hiding in the bushes at the edge of the forest, Schulze and Lore watched as the SS officer, followed by several 'chained dogs', machine pistols cradled in their arms, advanced on the little camp. The two watchers couldn't see his face, but they did see he carried his pistol in his right hand. Instinctively Schulze knew the officer was unpredictable, dangerous. Fervently he prayed that Matz would be able to come up with some plausible story for their being there. Perhaps the presence of the wounded CO and the crackpot medical general with his snow-white beard might lend some strength to whatever yarn he could dream up. Schulze hoped so. If not . . . He frowned and gripped his own weapon more tightly. But *that* would be pretty nip and tuck. They were outnumbered by about ten to one.

Matz gasped with shock. Even in the growing gloom of the July evening it wasn't difficult to recognize who the pasty-faced SS officer with the old-fashioned pince-nez was. It was the Creeper. Naturally he had survived the debacle at Caen. The Creepers of this world, Matz told himself, always came out of the shit smelling of roses. Slowly he started to rise to his feet and come to the position of attention.

But the Creeper had no eyes for the one-legged corporal. Face glowing with sudden triumph, he stared down at the wounded man cradled in the arms of the French civilian woman and exclaimed, 'You, at last, you arrogant bastard – Kuno von Dodenburg!' The Creeper shook violently, as if he were losing control over himself. 'I have you at last,' he said, talking to himself, overcome by a burning sense of rage as well as triumph. 'Now what can you do? Wounded, helpless, in my power, and yet finding pretty women to pander to you.'

Abruptly he couldn't control himself. Years of resentment – his life as a small-town schoolteacher; the glasses he was forced to wear; the fact that he had never received any medals for bravery in all his years in the SS, loyal as he was to the Führer; the betrayals of his wife, who had left him in the lurch when he had needed her most – rose up inside him and seemed to focus his hatred on the wounded colonel who was at his mercy, his absolute mercy. With a savage gesture, he ripped open his flies with one hand, keeping his pistol aimed at the little group, and pulled out his penis. Before anyone could stop him, he started to urinate over the unconscious man's body in a final gesture of his contempt, face twisted with hatred.

'*Non,*' Nurse Bogex cried . . . '*Non, ça suffit*—' Her protest ended in howl of pain as one of the 'chained dogs' kicked her savagely in the face with his heavy nailed boot and she reeled back, bleeding and dizzy.

'You bastard!' Matz attempted to dash forward and hit the man, but stopped in his tracks when the other 'chained dog' raised his weapon threateningly and clicked off the safety catch, growling, 'Do you want to die immediately, you front-swine bastard?'

Schulze knew the time had come to act. There was no alternative. Cost what it may, the Creeper had to die for the perverted manner that he had insulted the helpless CO. Next to him, Lore pressed his arm and said with genuine emotion, 'You've got to kill him – after that.'

Schulze said nothing. He clicked over to 'single shot'. He took the Creeper in his sights as he towered above von Dodenburg, who was beginning to stir and moan, his flaccid organ dangling from his breeches, a picture of jackbooted power and dominance, savouring the act, though he didn't quite know why, save that it gave him unspeakable satisfaction; it was almost like sexual pleasure.

Schulze aimed carefully. Suddenly the Creeper's ugly, bespectacled face was dissected by the cross hairs of the weapon. For what seemed too long a time, Schulze focused on it, as if he were etching every feature on his mind's eye for all eternity. Slowly he started to squeeze the trigger. He reached first pressure. He paused. He took a careful breath, forcing himself to suppress his hatred. He had to be calm. He completed the pressure. The weapon exploded. The butt slammed into his shoulder – hard. Fire spat from the muzzle. Next instant the hated face of von Dodenburg's tormentor disintegrated into a gory mess of bright-red blood through which the shattered bone gleamed like polished ivory. The Creeper gave a muffled scream as he choked in his blood. Next moment he was falling forward, dead before he hit the earth.

It was then that the dive-bombers came screaming in at 300 m.p.h., screeching over the trees, thrashing their branches into a wild green maelstrom, their cannon spitting white fury at the parked vehicles, and all disappeared into a crazy confusion of running men, dead men, burning vehicles, from which only those whom God loved could hope to survive . . .

ENVOI

'If only our generals had been as you.'
A. Hitler,
April 22nd, 1945

B ehind them, they left the wreckage of a German army: guns abandoned, with the barrels blown up; heavy tractors stalled for lack of fuel; huge Mercedes mobile workshops, fitted with electric lathes, automatic welders, priceless and highly modern; dental trucks; mobile film units; dredgers; French cars piled with the loot of four years of occupation; bodies . . .

For nearly three weeks, the worn, ragged little group had been on the run after their surprising escape from certain death when the Tommy *Jabos* had caught the 'chained dogs'' half-tracks completely by surprise. Time and time again they had survived death or capture. For it seemed half of Europe wanted its revenge now that the Germans were on the run. Death and destruction had come from the sky with the Typhoons withdrawing from their low-level attack to be replaced almost immediately by the Spitfires, cannon spurting white tracer shells, shooting up anything, machine or man, that moved on the ground below.

Death had come from behind the stone walls of the villages or the hedgerows of the countryside. Boys and old men in the *bleus de travail* of the French worker took potshots at the fugitives when it was safe to do so and then withdrew to their hiding places. Over the frontier into Belgium and it had been the young men of the *Witte Brigade* who had taken up the challenge to kill the *Moppen*. Clad in their white overalls, armed with the Sten guns the British had dropped them by parachute, they roamed the Belgian country lanes and side roads looking for solitary or unwary Germans to murder in the name of patriotism.

They had lost the big medical corps truck to the men of the 'White Brigade'. A burst of Sten-gun fire from behind a barn had ripped its engine apart and that had been that. They had marched on, carrying just as much as they could safely carry. That same day the old general with the white beard had collapsed and refused to go on any further. 'It's no use, comrades,' he croaked while Nurse Bogex tried to help. 'I can't go on. Leave me.' He coughed thickly and, standing around him, on the verge, they could hear the liquid which was filling his old lungs gurgle.

Weakly he had pushed the nurse's hand away and had quavered, 'But my pistol, please . . . I'd like to die like a soldier, if I can.'

Wordlessly Schulze, who was in charge, placed the loaded pistol on his chest, clicking off the safety for the old general. He grasped it gratefully. 'The officer's way out . . . if nothing else.' He tried to smile, but failed lamentably.

Lore started to cry softly and Nurse Bogex, taking von Dodenburg by the arm, began to lead him up the dead straight road. Schulze brought up the rear. He had cast one last look over his shoulder. The old general was lying there in the verge, perfectly still, but his hand still grasping the pistol. A few minutes later they heard the crack of the pistol like a dry twig snapping underfoot on a hot summer's day. The general had taken the 'officer's way out'.

Thereafter they had kept close to the Franco-Belgian border, heading for the Ardennes forest. There, hiding and waiting for darkness, they had witnessed an attempt by a sizeable German unit to cross the Meuse, being attacked by both planes and *Ami* Sherman tanks. It had been a ghastly affair. The shot-up vehicles, tanks, horses, men, had tumbled down into the deep gorge of the great river and had been jumbled together in gruesome heaps.

By nightfall the German attempt to cross had failed totally.

Hidden in the undergrowth of the chalky left bank of the Meuse, the fugitives watched as the rest gave in. Hundreds of them. The shuffling wrecks, hands raised, bowed with fatigue, although they had nothing to carry but their ragged uniforms and weary, hopeless battle-drugged bodies, advanced before the grinning, happy GIs, chewing gum like so many cattle chewing their cud. 'Bastards!' Schulze growled, his red-rimmed eyes angry. 'They think they've shitting well beaten us . . . Why I'd like to castrate the shitting lot of them with a blunt razor blade.'

Matz pressed his old comrade's arm. 'They have beaten us, Schulzi,' he said quietly. 'No two ways about it. Just let's look after ourselves, comrade.'

Listening to them, still unable to see much but a vague blur, von Dodenburg told himself that Matz was right. Yet they were the elite – the last survivors of SS Assault Regiment Wotan. Could they just give in like that? Von Dodenburg had had no answer for that overwhelming question. 'Why should you have?' a harsh little voice had rasped at the back of his mind. 'You're blind, aren't you? A cripple, of no more use to yourself or Germany.'

They crossed the Meuse without too much difficulty, taking the back roads and forest trails through the rugged Belgian Ardennes, telling themselves that once they were out of the Walloon area of the little country, they'd be safer. Then they'd be in the German-speaking cantons of the East – St. Vith, Eupen, Malmedy. They had been German, too, since 1940. Surely they'd find some refuge there.

But they weren't going to escape from French-speaking Belgium unscathed. Like their own little band, there were other groups of desperate Germans trying to reach the safety of the border and the Siegfried Line and the young fanatics of the Belgian underground army knew it. They were eager for the kill, ready to vent their pent-up frustration and anger of the occupation years on any German unlucky enough to fall into their hands; and unlike the grinning, gum-chewing

Americans on the River Meuse they weren't inclined to take prisoners.

Thus it was as Schulze's group was about to leave the French-speaking part, taking the back road from Bastogne to Houffalize on the border with the Reich, that they walked straight into a trap.

It was a bright summer's morning, with just a trace of a heat haze in the hills beyond, when Matz in the lead (followed by the two women and von Dodenburg, Schulze bringing up the rear) spotted the sudden bright light coming from the cobbled yard of the scruffy little farmhouse to his right. He had had his eye on the place since he had first seen it, noting the lazy curl of blue smoke coming from its chimney and the skinny cows grazing in the pasture beyond. Idly he wondered why there was no customary barking of the farmer's dog. Out here, all the farmers seemed to keep hounds which barked hysterically whenever a stranger came in sight. Up to now he had not paid the absence of a dog any great attention, but that sudden reflection and flash of light made him frown. There was someone there obviously, but why hadn't that someone made an appearance in the cobbled, manure-filled yard to the front of the house? Usually these farmers were out like a shot when a stranger appeared, worried that the newcomer might want to steal their eggs or sides of bacon hanging up under the rafters inside their tumbledown farms.

Matz made a quick decision. 'M'lle Bogex, get the Colonel into that ditch over there and keep your head down . . . Schulze, watch it.'

'What's the matter, Corporal?' von Dodenburg began, but Nurse Bogex didn't give him a chance to finish. She pushed him into the ditch. He fell heavily, and cried out.

No one heard. For already a light machine gun had opened up from the direction of the farm where Matz had seen the light flash, and tracer was zipping towards them in a lethal Morse. Old hares that they were, Schulze and Matz dropped to the ground and started to return the fire with short, sharp bursts of their automatics, conserving their ammunition, for they had little left after all this time. At the same time, they waited for other weapons to open up. For they realized that the partisans, if that was what they were, had spotted them coming and had prepared a proper ambush.

The two veterans were right. Automatic fire now commenced to their rear.

That meant they had two choices. They could stay where they were, remain pinned down until they ran out of ammo, or they could make a run for it to their front. But to their front the road ran up a steep hill. They'd never make it, hindered as they were by a sick officer and two women. But Matz and Schulze had not survived this long war by doing the expected. They had soon learned in the early battles in Russia that in an ambush, you did the unexpected, tried to catch the enemy off guard and wipe him out before he could recover.

Matz cupped his hands around his mouth and yelled above the *brr-brr* of the enemy automatic fire, 'Schulzi!'

'*Ja?*'

'D'yer hear. Flankers left and right. *Dalli . . . Dalli!*'

'With your peg leg, you Bavarian barnshitter?'

'You watch me go, arse-with-ears.'

'*Einverstanden . . . Eins, zwei, drei. JETZT!*'

Abruptly they were on their feet, running for all they were worth, heading straight into the enemy fire coming from the farm, going on all out, zig-zagging the best they could, their slugs slamming into the brickwork around the tiny windows, knowing that the enemy would be disconcerted by fire coming straight at them. After all they weren't the elite of SS Assault Regiment Wotan, veterans of the battles of Kursk, Leningrad and Stalingrad; they were just crappy civilians who had been handed a gun and told how to fire it.

The tactic worked. Behind them the other automatic ceased firing; obviously the gunner didn't want to hit his own people in the farm. Safe from that quarter, the two attackers slammed into the wall near the door inside the 'dead ground' where they couldn't really be seen from inside the rundown farm.

They gulped for breath. Schulze gave the usual hand signals. Matz drew his last stick grenade from his boot. He pulled out the china pin. Schulze waited an instant, counting off three, and kicked open the door. Matz flung in the grenade. Schulze pulled the door tightly closed again and held on to the handle with all his strength. A second's pause. *Crump!* A muffled explosion from inside the farm. The door heaved. Glass cracked and tinkled to the floor. Next instant Schulze had ripped the door off its sagging hinges and was inside, spraying the interior from left to right with slugs. A cry of pain, a curse. A heavy body fell from the top of the stairs and hit the tiles of the entrance like a sack of wet cement.

Minutes later it was all over.

Schulze and Matz, flushed and jittery, didn't waste any more time on the farmhouse. They knew there'd be more of the partisans arriving on the scene soon; the gunner to the rear would be informing them of what had happened already probably. Hastily they searched the house for the paraffin the peasants used to fuel their lamps. They found it, splashed it everywhere on the wooden chairs and benches of the kitchen and fired the place into a swift burst of flame. In seconds the farmhouse was burning merrily, its half-timbered frame already well alight. It was their revenge. But they didn't wait to savour it. '*Los . . . los marsch, marsch!*' Schulze yelled, pumping his fist up and down rapidly in the infantry signal for swift movement. It had been then that the two old hares discovered that Lore was missing, and that von Dodenburg could see again . . .

Holed up that night on a wooden hillside just to the east of the border town of Houffalize, the German frontier only a matter of kilometres away, von Dodenburg explained, 'I don't know how it happened. I think when I was pushed into the ditch back there, it must have done the trick. I've heard of such things.' He rubbed his eyes, as if he were making quite sure that his sight had really returned.

'And the girl – Lore?' Nurse Bogex's delight at this miraculous cure was tinged with a certain sadness as she thought of the missing Lore.

Matz shrugged unhappily. 'They'll rape her first – all of them. Partisans always take their revenge first on the womenfolk. And then . . .' He didn't finish. Instead he crooked his dirty forefinger, as if he were pulling the trigger of a pistol. '*Fini la grande guerre.*'

Schulze remembered Lore with her legs up in the air or around his neck, gasping like a stranded fish, begging him to 'pump it to her', and remarked in his customary sentimental fashion, 'She *was* a good fuck . . .'

'Is that the way all soldiers think of women?' Nurse Bogex asked later as she and von Dodenburg were alone, staring down at the silver sheen of the River Our, the frontier river, far below. 'What did Sergeant Schulze say? "A good fuck."' She stared at von Dodenburg, her dark eyes full of love.

'I suppose they do.' Von Dodenburg took his eyes off the stream and bunkers built into the bank beyond. They seemed empty. Indeed the whole countryside appeared empty of German troops. Had the defenders of the Westwall* fled even before the *Amis* arrived to attack its fortifications? 'We live such short, brutal lives. I don't think we have time for love.' He shrugged. 'I suppose that's the way with us.'

'You have known a lot of women?' she asked after a few moments.

He nodded. 'I've not exactly been a monk in these last years. The nature of the beast, you know. Why do you ask?'

'It's obvious, isn't it?' she said in that direct fashion of hers.

He looked at her face in the spectral light of the sickle

*Westwall, called the Siegfried Line by the Western Allies. *Transl.*

moon. 'But you're French and I'm German. Technically we're enemies.' He pressed her hand swiftly and softened the statement with, 'Of course I know we aren't. I owe a lot to you, perhaps even my life. But what future can there be for us in whatever future there is for an SS officer in a conquered Germany?'

'I would wait for you.' Abruptly her voice seemed to break and he felt she was close to tears. 'They'd have to let you out sometime, if they did imprison you.'

He frowned. She was making him think of the future when he didn't want to, because he didn't believe he had one; and in a way he didn't want to survive in a defeated Germany. By now his command had vanished. All his old hares were dead or behind the barbed wire of the Allied prisoner-of-war camps. It was the same with most of his friends, who had joined the SS with such high hopes back in the late thirties, believing they were the young elite who would put an end to the old decadent Europe governed by ancient crooks and replace it with a cleaner, fresher 'New Order'. They had long vanished in battlefields all over Europe. Now it seemed they had died for nothing. It would be an act of betrayal if he attempted to make a nice comfortable bourgeois future for himself. He simply couldn't visualize himself as a plump papa with happy children, leading a slippered, domesticated existence, supported by a loving, adoring even, *Hausfrau*, who produced another child regularly every year.

'You are not saying anything,' she said after a while, withdrawing her hand from his grasp. 'Why, Kuno?'

He roused himself from his reverie. 'Because I don't think there's anything to say. I don't think I can plan a future further than getting over the River Our down there safely—'

He never finished his explanation. Over to the right dark shapes were beginning to slink through the firs. Soft voices spoke in English and French. Now in the distance he heard the rumble of tank tracks – American tanks, for these tracks were coated with rubber as the *Ami* tanks were. He grasped what was going in immediately. These were the men of the *Ami* vanguard. They had made contact with the local Belgian resistance and were using the latter to guide them through the dense forest down to the border river. By morning, he guessed, they'd be up on the heights here in full force, massing to attack into the Siegfried Line – and the Siegfried Line in this area seemed to be totally undefended. The German authorities had to be warned.

He rose, putting his finger to his lips to warn her to be careful. 'Come,' he whispered. *'Die Amis sind da!'*

For a moment she hesitated, as if she wondered whether she should go with him. But her love for the harshly handsome SS colonel was too great. She rose, too. Five minutes later the four of them were scrambling and slipping down the slate-lined bank of the little border river and what lay beyond . . .

In nearby Bitburg, filled with hundreds of stragglers from a dozen different units, they had been welcomed with open arms. The harassed town commander, an elderly colonel wearing the medal ribbons of the First World War, had seemed about to kiss Kuno von Dodenburg when he reported in with *'Obersturmbannführer von Dodenburg vom Sturmregiment Wotam meldet sich zur Stelle!'* Even the fact that the SS officer's regiment seemed to consist of only two NCOs and a French nurse didn't seemed to worry him unduly.

'My dear Colonel,' the town commander had gushed, 'you come like an answer to a virgin's prayer. I've got the men . . . I've got the weapons . . . I've got transport. All I haven't got is an officer with some guts to command them, once I can get them to man the Westwall line.'

'Well, now you've got a leader, *Herr Oberst*,' von Dodenburg had replied enthusiastically. Abruptly he had felt the adrenaline flowing, powered by the kind of fervour that had motivated him back in the great days of victory after victory when SS Assault Regiment Wotan had smashed its way across Europe, virtually unstoppable, before it had been chased and chivvied too long by the enemy, all the way from the damned D-Day beaches across half of Northern Europe back to the homeland, harassed by those overweening Anglo-Americans, with their overwhelming superiority in men and materiel. Now the time had come to show them once again how the German soldier could fight, especially as he was fighting on his own soil.

That dawn he had formed his mixed bag of stragglers and deserters and reluctant heroes into alarm companies, each a hundred men strong, commanded by anyone who volunteered to do so. Now second lieutenants and simple sergeants with fire in their bellies commanded companies made up of fat-bellied staff captains and majors. Rank didn't count any more, only guts.

Once, as he was loading them into the waiting trucks, their drivers gunning their engines as if they couldn't get started quickly enough, he had caught a glimpse of Nurse Bogex. She had been crying, but she was safe. They were sending her to the nearby military hospital at Trier. She'd be well looked after there, the old colonel had assured him. She had waved wanly and had then allowed the soldiers to heave her into the ambulance filled with wounded which would take her to the place. It moved off. She didn't turn again. For a moment he had registered the parting from this Frenchwoman who loved him even to the point of turning traitor to her own country. Then he had dismissed her from his mind. The front had been calling.

Now they were in position between Stolzembourg and Steinebruck. The old bunkers and pillboxes of the Westwall, which had been abandoned back in 1940 after the great victory over the west, were once again filled with men in the field-grey of the Greater German *Wehrmacht*. Rapidly they had cleared away the undergrowth that had blocked the old fields of fire. New barbed wire had been strung. Cannon again poked their long snouts through the apertures, manned by these hastily flung-together alarm companies, composed of soldiers of a dozen different arms of the service. There were even a handful of sailors and marines among them.

Suddenly there was a new hope in the air. Back in '40, the Tommies had sung how they were 'going to hang out the washing on the Siegfried Line'. They had never done so. Instead they had been chased right across the French plain and had been flung headlong out of the Continent at Dunkirk, never to return till now. Perhaps that might happen again? Even the poorest soldier, fighting from behind two metres of concrete, was the match for half a dozen *Amis* or Tommies advancing across open fields with no cover to protect them; and even if the enemy did take the bunkers, they would have to do so at terrible cost. They'd soon get weary of the enormous casualties. Perhaps Germany might get a more favourable peace after all?

Kuno von Dodenburg believed so. Flanked by Schulze and Matz, he peered through the forward bunker's periscope as the first khaki-clad shapes came out of the trees and began to wade the thigh-deep River Our cautiously, their weapons held high. Next to him Schulze said, 'Look at the piss-pansies. They think they've got it all tied up. Germany's finished and it's going to be a walkover.' Suddenly he was overcome by an unreasoning rage. He seized his MG42 and slammed the butt into his shoulder as if it were a child's toy. He pressed the trigger. The weapon burst into frenzied activity. The Americans went down everywhere and Schulze cried, 'Try that on for size, you American bastards . . . WELCOME TO OLD GERMANY!'

The six-month-long battle for the German frontier had commenced . . .